"Ah, hell," he muttered. ... Trish? A plant? A willing player in his mother's scheme to marry him off?

Or was she just a pawn?

Adam pushed away from his desk and began to pace. He stopped. Shook his head. Paced some more. Stopped again.

He was driving himself crazy.

Maybe it was just a happy coincidence that his previous secretary had left the company, replaced by a certain attractive woman who just might be capable of seducing him into love and marriage.

His eyes narrowed as he conjured up a picture of his mother meeting, scheming, conniving to pull it off.

Suddenly, it didn't seem at all far-fetched.

He had to hand it to them, he admitted with a short laugh. It was a nice try. Trish was definitely attractive. But while he might enjoy the seduction part, there was no way in hell he'd fall for the whole marriage package.

Dear Reader,

I'm thrilled to welcome you to my first Silhouette Desire! I've been a Desire reader for years, so it's a dream come true for me to be writing for them.

The saying goes "man plans and God laughs." Well, this is a story of the best laid plans going awry. Trish James devises a simple plan of revenge when she goes to work for Adam Duke. She holds Adam responsible for destroying her home and family, and she'll stop at nothing to ruin him. Or so she thinks.

Adam has big plans, too, none of which includes marriage. But seduction? Absolutely. But as his desire for Trish grows, so does his suspicion that his mother might've had something to do with Trish getting the job. This mom is not above scheming and matchmaking if it means her three handsome sons will fall in love, marry and give her lots of grandbabies to love. So what happens when the plans of a vengeful secretary, a seductive millionaire and a matchmaking mama collide? Sparks fly, to say the least!

I hope you love reading Adam and Trish's story as much as I loved writing it. Let me know! You can reach me through my Web site, www.katecarlisle.com.

Happy reading!

Kate

KATE CARLISLE

THE MILLIONAIRE MEETS HIS MATCH

Published by Silhouette Books
America's Publisher of Contemporary Romance

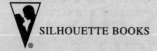

SILHOUETTE BOOKS

ISBN-13: 978-0-373-73036-0

Recycling programs
for this product may
not exist in your area.

THE MILLIONAIRE MEETS HIS MATCH

KATE CARLISLE

New York Times bestselling author Kate Carlisle was born and raised by the beach in Southern California. After more than twenty years in television production, Kate turned to writing the types of mysteries and romance novels she always loved to read. She still lives by the beach in Southern California with her husband, and when they're not taking long walks in the sand or cooking or reading or painting or taking bookbinding classes or trying to learn a new language, they're traveling the world, visiting family and friends in the strangest places. Kate loves to hear from readers. Visit her Web site at www.katecarlisle.com.

To my fellow Desire author Maureen Child,
a marvelously talented writer and a truly wonderful
friend. I couldn't have done it without you…
and the lattes…and the doughnuts…the laughs…
and the trips to Vegas…and so much more. Love you!

One

"Consider this fair warning. Watch your back or I guarantee they'll take you down."

"You're making too much of this," Adam Duke said as he eased his black Ferrari into his parking space near the executive entrance of Duke Development International.

"You think so?" His brother Brandon's voice came through loud and clear over the car's state-of-the-art sound system. "I'll be sure to remind you of that after you've said your wedding vows and promised to live happily ever after with the girl of *Mom's* dreams."

"You need to chill out," Adam said. He shifted into Park and grabbed his briefcase before stepping out of his car.

"Hey, it's your funeral," Brandon groused. "Or wedding. Whatever. Just don't be surprised when you find yourself on a honeymoon with some woman who was planted right under your nose by our diabolically clever mother."

Adam laughed as he took a moment to straighten his tie before strolling inside. The ultramodern office building he owned with his brothers, Cameron and Brandon, was the headquarters of Duke Development International. "I think I'm safe," Adam said. "The chances of Mom sneaking anything past me while I'm working twenty-two hours a day on this closing are pretty slim."

His brother, Cameron, also in on the three-way conference call, spoke for the first time. "Despite Brandon's typical overkill, you know Mom. She's relentless. She thinks we should all be married and now she's playing hardball. That means she'll try every devious trick in the book to make it happen."

"Right, that's all I'm saying," Brandon said, apparently relieved that at least one of his brothers was getting the message.

"Okay," Cameron said. "Might be a good idea to stay alert for the time being."

"Yeah, be alert for the skirt," Brandon said, then added with a snicker, "or you could get hurt."

The brothers shared a laugh at Brandon's pitiful attempt at poetry.

"Look, I'll see you guys later," Adam said. "We can finish this conversation then."

Still chuckling, Adam disconnected the call and waved to the DDI security guard who stood at attention next to the wide, polished marble registration desk in the lavishly appointed lobby. He stepped inside an empty elevator car and ascended alone to the penthouse floor.

The fact that his mother was trying to set up Adam and his brothers was no surprise. She'd made it eminently clear on any number of occasions that she wanted grandchildren. But now Brandon was making it sound as if she were suddenly on a crusade and willing to use underhanded means to introduce new women into their lives.

"Take your best shot, Mom," Adam murmured as he made his way down the broad, open corridor toward the executive offices. He loved Sally Duke, the woman who'd adopted him when he was eight years old, but Adam Duke was the last person on earth who would succumb to her machinations when it came to marriage.

Whistling softly, he walked past his assistant's empty chair, noticed that her computer wasn't turned on yet, and marveled that he'd actually made it into work before her this morning. That was rare. Cheryl Hardy was a workaholic who loved her job. A good thing, because they'd be working night and day for the rest of the month, right up to the evening of the gala grand opening of the new Duke resort at Fantasy Mountain.

"What do you mean, she *quit?*" Adam demanded an hour later. "My people don't quit."

"This one did," Marjorie Wallace, his long-time Human Resources manager said.

"Impossible. We're about to close on a billion-dollar deal." Adam pushed back from the massive mahogany desk and rose to pace along the wall of windows that overlooked the craggy coastline of Dunsmuir Bay and the clear blue ocean beyond. It was a breathtaking view of the central California coast, one he saw every day and never grew tired of, but it mattered little now as he whipped around to confront Marjorie. "She's not allowed to leave."

"Actually, she is. It's not like she was an indentured servant," the older woman said drily. "She's gone, Adam. Let's move on."

"Did she say why?" Adam raked one hand through his hair. "Never mind. I'll double her salary. We can work this out."

He didn't appreciate Marjorie's dry chuckle. "Oh, really?" the HR manager asked. "How many times did Cheryl remind you that she needed a vacation and you convinced her she didn't? She told you she was getting married. You brushed her off."

"She never said a word. I would've listened."

"She told you every day."

"She didn't," Adam insisted, although he had a vague memory of Cheryl mentioning...something...about a wedding. Had she been talking about her own wedding? He couldn't remember. It hadn't seemed important at the time.

"She did," Marjorie maintained defiantly.

Adam rounded the desk and faced the insolent woman up close. "You're not supposed to argue with the boss."

Marjorie's laugh rang out. "Oh, Adam."

Adam scowled. "Remind me again why I haven't fired you for insubordination."

"Let's see." Marjorie's grin remained as she folded her arms across her chest. "Maybe because I'm so darn good at my job? Or maybe because I'm your mother's best friend and I've known you since you were eight years old? Or could it be because I've never told your mother who really hit the baseball that broke her office window when you were nine or who trampled her prize tulips that same summer? Oh, and what about the time you were grounded and I caught you sneaking out to—"

"All right, all right," Adam said irately, holding up his hand for her to stop. "There should be a statute of limitations on that kind of stuff."

"Sorry," Marjorie said with a grin. "Honorary aunties never forget."

"Tell me about it," Adam muttered. "Look, this is ridiculous. Get Cheryl on the phone."

"She quit," Marjorie said, enunciating the words so he couldn't ignore them. "She won't be back. She was three months' pregnant and working around the clock. Something had to give."

He stopped in midpace and turned. "Pregnant?"

Marjorie nodded.

Appalled, he threw his hands up. "She always insisted she was a shark. She loved the kill. Sharks don't get pregnant and run off in the middle of a deal."

Marjorie shrugged. "I guess she was a dolphin in shark's clothing."

"Very funny," he said coldly. "You can't trust anyone these days."

"So true."

"I don't have time for this," Adam said abruptly. "I need a replacement, now."

Marjorie smiled. "I've got the perfect person for you."

Adam stopped her with a look. "I'm warning you, Marjorie. Don't bring me someone who's going to get pregnant and leave without notice."

"Of course not," she said with a huff.

"And I don't want some bubble-gum-chewing bobblehead doll." He stalked back and forth in front of the desk, warming to his rant. "I want someone with maturity, someone who knows the damn alphabet well enough to file something in the right drawer. And I definitely don't want—"

"I know what you want, boss," Marjorie said quickly. "And I've got just the person for you. Trish has gotten rave reviews as one of our best special assignment assistants. Her credentials are—"

"A floater?" Adam said, shaking his head in disbelief. "Are you kidding me?"

"Special assignment assistant," Marjorie said through clenched teeth.

He waved her off. "I won't work with a floater. This job's too important to trust—"

"We don't have a choice," Marjorie said with a hiss, then added in a normal tone, "Trish's credentials are excellent. She graduated from a very good college, then went on to get her MBA. She's smart as a whip. I think you'll be pleasantly surprised."

"How smart can she be if she's in the floater pool?" he said stubbornly.

Marjorie straightened her spine and pierced him with a look. "Our floaters—I mean, special assignment assistants—are top notch and you know it."

"Of course they are," he said. It was true. Duke's floaters were an enthusiastic and skilled group. But that wouldn't be enough for this job.

"Now, you behave," Marjorie added in a hushed voice, making Adam feel like a ten-year-old who'd been caught stealing apples from old man Petrie's orchard. "Trish is very smart and pretty."

"Yeah, but can she type?" Adam muttered acerbically.

* * *

Trish James had heard more than enough from Adam Duke, who obviously hadn't noticed that she'd been standing in the doorway to his office for the last five minutes.

It's showtime, she thought, steeling her nerves as she pushed away from the door and crossed the wide, elegantly furnished office to introduce herself.

"I type 120 words per minute, Mr. Duke," Trish said brightly as she held out her hand to shake Adam Duke's. "It's nice to meet you. I'm Trish James, your special assignment assistant."

As their hands touched, Trish felt a jolt of heat and stared up at the man, hoping her apprehension didn't show on her face. She'd known from the start that the CEO of Duke Development would be a formidable opponent. She just hadn't realized that he'd be so tall and intimidating. Or so attractive—if you cared for the sort of potent, masculine toughness that must've appealed to every last woman in the known universe. Looking into his dark blue eyes, she felt her stomach take an unwelcome dip. Even seething with anger, Adam oozed sex appeal from every inch of his broad, muscular frame. Minutes ago, as she'd watched him from the office doorway, Trish had had to stifle an almost overwhelming urge to sneak away.

But Grandma Anna hadn't raised a coward, so she'd pushed ahead and here she was, ready to beard the lion in his own den.

"Trish dear," Marjorie said with a wink, clearly aware that Trish had overheard everything the HR manager and Adam had just said. "This is Adam Duke, of course. You'll be working together for the next few weeks. I know you'll do a wonderful job. Call me if you have any questions."

Marjorie gave Adam a final warning glance, then smiled again. "Have a good day, both of you." Then she turned and raced toward the door.

Trish almost laughed. Sure, have a good day. It was really starting out well. She tracked Marjorie's escape out the door, leaving Trish on her own to face the man who had haunted her dreams for the last year. A man who'd turned those dreams to nightmares.

A man who didn't even know who she was.

"Welcome," Adam said gruffly.

"Thank you," Trish said graciously, ignoring the insincerity in both their voices. They'd just started off on the wrong foot. Determined to right the situation and conduct herself professionally, she cleared her throat and said, "I appreciate that you'd rather not depend on a floater, Mr. Duke, but let me assure you that I know my way around an office."

His eyes narrowed. "We refer to them as special assignment assistants, Ms. James."

It took her a moment to realize he was joking. "Of course we do. My mistake."

He smiled reluctantly. "That's better."

Her entire system zoomed up to red alert. It was that devastating smile that did it. *Warning!* her nerve endings screamed. In that moment, she could see how his former assistant might've been seduced into working for him until she snapped in two.

Determined to follow through with her plan, she squared her shoulders. Despite his gorgeous face, Adam Duke was a shark. He personified the killer species, and Trish ought to know, since he'd cold-bloodedly destroyed everything she'd ever loved. Now it was payback time. That's why she was here.

Looking at him now, she had to admit he was the best-looking shark she'd ever seen. His eyes sparkled with both awareness and cynicism, but Trish could imagine them turning to blue ice if he ever discovered her true reason for being here.

"Ms. James?"

"What? Yes?" Trish blinked. The last thing she needed was to be caught staring soulfully at her unforgiving boss. "I'm sorry, I was taking mental notes. Could you repeat that?"

With a thoughtful nod, he glanced at his watch. "I've got to leave for a meeting shortly, but I'll show you around first."

As they crossed the luxurious space, Adam pointed out the locked cabinet where he kept some personal files, next to a sideboard with coffee and sodas to which she could help herself.

"Thank you," she said. "I appreciate that."

"I'm not sure you will when you have no time to go to lunch and this is all you're stuck with."

"At least we won't die of thirst," she said lightheartedly, but her grin faded as she met his gaze and was struck again by his sheer strength and masculinity. She had to force herself to get a grip.

Despite his good looks, she knew he was inflexible and demanding, knew he would be a formidable taskmaster. Frankly, she wished she could tell him to take this job and…well, she couldn't say it. She needed the job too much. She was on a mission and she would accomplish what she'd set out to do. Let Adam Duke look down on her, if it made him feel bigger and better. She didn't care. The worse he treated her, the more justification she would have for doing what she'd come here to do.

But why did he have to be even more gorgeous in person than in the newspaper photographs she'd studied? Honestly, didn't she have enough to handle without being bombarded by feelings of attraction for a man who had single-handedly brought so much pain and destruction to her life?

No, it didn't matter how handsome he was. All that mattered was, if not for Adam Duke, Trish would still have her home and her grandmother would still be alive.

Adam checked his wristwatch again and Trish snapped back to attention. "I'm sorry, Mr. Duke, but I don't know your schedule yet. Do you need to leave for your meeting?"

"I'll be cutting it close," Adam said distractedly. "Let me get you settled before I go."

He led the way out to the large alcove where she would work. He pointed out the wall of file drawers behind her desk that held most of his clients' personal information and all the deals he was currently working on.

"Arranged in alphabetical order," he added.

Remembering his comment to the HR manager, Trish smiled. "I assure you I'm familiar with the alphabet."

He managed a rueful chuckle. "Let's hope so, Ms. James."

Trish grabbed a pad and took fast notes as he gave her a list of names of people whose calls he would always take, along with his cell phone number.

"While I'm gone, you can get your desk arranged, then I've left a cost analysis to be typed up, as well as some other letters and documents that need revisions.

If you have time, you can start studying what's inside those file drawers. I'll need the Mansfield papers when I get back."

Trish wrote everything down, then smiled. "I'll take care of everything, Mr. Duke. You won't be sorry."

With a look that said he was already sorry, he said, "Call me Adam."

"And please call me Trish," she said.

"Right." He looked at her for a moment, his mouth set in a skeptical scowl.

She smiled expectantly.

"Don't forget the Mansfield papers," he said finally, then strolled out of the executive suite, leaving Trish more shaken than she wanted to admit.

"That went well," Adam muttered in disgust as he pounded the elevator call button. "Knucklehead."

As he contemplated the attractive brunette who was now assigned to be his interim assistant, three things bothered him. First, the woman had been able to sneak up on him without him even noticing, and that never happened. He attributed his lack of awareness to his angry reaction to the news that his formerly invaluable assistant had run off and left him in a bind.

It had been obvious by her sardonic smile as they shook hands that Trish James had heard every word of his tirade over Cheryl's untimely departure—and that was the second thing that bothered him. No one ever saw Adam Duke lose his cool. His control was legendary. Marjorie didn't count. He'd known the woman for almost as long as he'd known his adoptive mother.

But now Trish James had seen him ranting like an idiot and that was never a good way to begin a working relationship—not that they would have that lengthy a working relationship, he hastened to add. He would need someone much more highly qualified to take over the position of executive assistant, not some refugee from the floater pool.

He immediately backed away from that thought. Marjorie was right, the floaters in his company were all good workers with great attitudes, willing to pitch in wherever they were needed. But Adam would need someone with top skills and experience, a self-starter and a go-getter with enthusiasm for the long work hours and a deft hand at dealing with his very demanding clients.

The third thing that bothered him was that she didn't look like the usual matronly floater his company employed. Notwithstanding that mocking little grin, her mouth was a bit too wide and her lips too lush. Her almond-shaped, dark green eyes seemed to focus a little too knowingly on him. He'd noticed the confidence in her posture and the way she held her chin high, and found himself grudgingly admiring her. She seemed determined to make this work.

She wore her shiny, chestnut-brown hair pulled back from her face in a classic style, and her black, pin-striped pantsuit fit her tall, poised figure like a glove. He generally hated pantsuits on women, but hers wasn't so bad. If his instincts were right, and they usually were, Trish James's suit covered one fantastic set of legs.

His groin tightened uncomfortably at the thought and he smacked the elevator button again. Her touch had sent something hot and wicked blasting through him and Adam wasn't about to encourage it.

But hell, every time she'd smiled up at him, Adam had felt his pulse spike. Her eyes had glittered with natural humor and her smiling lips were moist and full.

"And you hightailed it out of there like you were being chased by the town bully," he muttered in annoyance as the elevator doors finally opened. Two tech guys exiting gave him a puzzled look, but he ignored them both as he stepped inside.

It was just as well that he'd rushed out of the office, he thought as the elevator descended to the lobby. It would've been a lot worse if he'd stuck around and she'd happened to notice the bulging evidence of his desire for her.

Adam rubbed his hand along his jaw in frustration. What the hell was wrong with him? He wasn't some hormone-driven kid out on a date with the prom queen. This was just lust, pure and simple, and easily conquered. He wouldn't be led around by his libido. Ever.

Shoving open the private entry door leading out to the parking lot, Adam realized what this sudden attack of lust was all about. He'd been working day and night for months in anticipation of closing the Fantasy Mountain resort deal. He just needed to get the job done, then he needed to get laid. And not by one of his own employees, he added silently. There were any number of willing women he could call for a night of casual sex. And he would. As soon as he closed the deal.

As he jumped into the driver's seat of the Ferrari, he remembered his earlier conversation with Brandon and Cameron. Something about Mom trying every trick in the book to set him up with a marriage-minded woman.

An image of Trish James flashed through his mind and Adam frowned. Okay, that was ridiculous. There was no way his mother had anything to do with Trish being hired. Yes, the timing was a bit coincidental, and

Adam didn't believe in coincidences. But the idea was ludicrous.

He turned the key and listened to the finely tuned, high-performance engine roar to life. It was beyond ridiculous to imagine his mother going to that much trouble. He realized that he was buying into Brandon's paranoia and he shook it off.

But, meanwhile, he would do everything he could to avoid spending too much time with the gorgeous brunette who seemed destined, through no fault of her own, to make his calm and ordered life a living hell.

After a quick glass of water and a few cleansing breaths, Trish was ready to get to work. After all, she was being paid well and her work ethic was strong, so just because she was out to ruin the man didn't mean she wouldn't do a good job for him while she was here.

She started by exploring her new workspace. It was bright and spacious, just outside the doors to Adam Duke's palatial office. Everything was big and impressive, befitting the executive assistant to the president and CEO of Duke Development International.

The cherrywood desk was almost as big as her apartment's actual living room. And while it wasn't quite as dramatic as the floor-to-ceiling view of the coast from Adam's office, Trish actually had a view of the ocean from the window directly across from her desk. If she wasn't careful, she could get used to all this extravagance.

"But you *will* be careful," she admonished herself. She wasn't here to get comfortable, to enjoy any perks of the job. Just as she wasn't here to sigh over Adam Duke like some starstruck teenager.

But really, why couldn't the guy look like a troll?

"Let it go, Trish," she said, rolling her eyes. "Just get to work."

Forty minutes later, after she'd finished revising Adam's letters and documents and completed the cost analysis he'd left, Trish faced the file drawers. She wasn't even sure what she was looking for, but the faster she found something incriminating inside these drawers, the faster she'd be able to give up this sham job and be on her way. Maybe she would find what she needed today. That would certainly save her from weeks of turmoil, working side by side with the most delectable man on the planet.

"He even smells good," she groused, recalling his subtle scent that reminded her of green forests and autumn rain. "You weren't going to dwell on that, remember?"

Resolutely she opened the first drawer and began to sort through the files. An hour later, after memorizing every client name from A to M, Trish came to the Mansfield file, the one Adam had requested. He still wasn't back from his meeting so she looked through the file, studied the issues involved in the deal, then laid the thick folder on Adam's desk.

Finished with the tasks he'd assigned her, Trish checked her e-mail, printed her list of job priorities. She vowed to be on time every day and to do her job to the best of her ability while creating a pleasant work environment for everyone around her. She would make herself an invaluable member of Adam's team.

And then she would destroy him.

Two

"I'm telling you, the woman's gone off the deep end with this marriage thing." Brandon Duke paced in front of the Dunsmuir Bay Yacht Club's wide bay window, ignoring the picture-perfect view of sailboats and blue skies lying beyond the glass. "She's obsessed."

"Why is that a surprise?" Adam grinned, then took a quick sip of strong coffee. "And why are you so freaked out? It's not like this is the first time Mom's tried to talk us into getting married. She wants grandkids and we're not cooperating."

"That's right," his brother, Cameron, said, sitting back in the comfortable captain's chair. Despite the thousand-dollar business suit and silk designer necktie, Cameron looked completely relaxed. But Adam knew he never relaxed. A former Marine, Cameron was more driven, possibly more ruthless, than anyone Adam had ever known. Except himself.

"Remember when she forced us all to watch videos of her wedding day?" Cameron asked, shaking his head. "She thought it would soften us up or something."

"That was gruesome," Brandon agreed. "But the wedding cake looked good." He stretched his wide shoulders, glanced around the busy dining room, then sat down at the table and studied the yacht club breakfast menu. "Are we eating or what?"

"Are we breathing?" Adam said with a laugh.

"You're always eating," Cameron said to Brandon as he picked up the menu.

Brandon ignored his older brothers and signaled the waitress over. "I'll have pancakes, eggs and bacon. And toast. Better make it a double order of toast."

"I'll have the Denver omelet," Cameron said, and set the menu down. "And throw in a short stack, will you, Janie?"

"You bet, Mr. Duke," Janie, the waitress, said. She turned to Adam. "How about you, Mr. Duke?"

"I'll stick with coffee," Adam said. He needed the jolt to snap him out of the knee-jerk reaction he'd had to his new temporary assistant earlier. If he'd been more awake, she never would've caught him so off guard.

Janie poured more coffee, then scurried off.

Brandon said solemnly, "Look, guys, about Mom. This time it's different. She's serious. You should've heard her on the phone with her pal, Beatrice. She's lined up a whole squadron of friends to work on this thing. They've already got women lined up for each of us."

"Oh, yeah?" Cameron said with a leer. "I'm always on the lookout for new women. Remind me to thank her when I see her this weekend."

Adam raised an eyebrow. "If you really want to

date someone Mom picked out, there's always Susie Walton."

Cameron shivered visibly at the high school memory. "Why'd you have to go and spoil my appetite like that?"

"That's my job." Adam turned to Brandon. "Did you tell her you're on to her?"

"Hell, no," Brandon said. "The woman's a runaway train and I don't feel like getting flattened."

"Smart." Adam stared out at a sailboat passing by under motor power until it made its way into the marina channel. He shook his head. "What makes her think I'd marry any woman she threw at me?"

"Good question," Brandon said, stymied.

"What makes her think we'd marry *anyone,* ever?" Cameron said.

"She's Mom," Brandon said with a shrug.

"Yeah." Cameron sighed. "She's like a heat-seeking missile when she gets a bug up her butt."

"Interesting mixed metaphor," Adam said as he lifted his coffee cup. "But apropos nonetheless."

Cameron shot Adam a look of derision. "Dude, apropos? Nonetheless?"

Brandon slugged Cameron's arm. "Leave him alone. He's using his words."

Cameron snorted. "Right. Sorry."

Adam disregarded them. "The bottom line is, she's not setting me up," Adam said easily.

"That's my point," Brandon persisted. "She's not setting anyone up. It's going to be a surprise attack this time. She told Beatrice, and I quote, 'They won't know what hit them.'"

His two brothers shared a look of amusement, but

Brandon wasn't cowed. He shook his finger at Adam. "Ignore me at your peril, dude."

Adam glanced at Cameron, who raised his eyebrows at his brother's adamant tone but said nothing.

Brandon saw the exchange and held up his hands. "I'm just saying, watch out. You're first on her list, Adam. And if you fall…"

"I won't," Adam said.

"Good luck," Brandon grumbled. "The woman's diabolical."

Cameron took a sip of coffee, then wiped an imaginary tear from his eye. "It'll be so poignant watching Adam tie the knot."

Brandon grinned and joined in with a few fake sniffles. "Our little guy's all grown up."

"Very funny," Adam said tightly. "I'm not tying anything." He looked from Cameron to Brandon. "And neither are you two. We made a pact."

The men grew silent as Adam's words took them back to the day when three eight-year-old boys were forced to make peace with each other. They'd been fighting all morning until their foster mother, Sally Duke, had had enough. She put sandwiches, chips and boxes of juice up in the custom tree house she'd had built for them and warned them not to come down until they could learn to live as brothers.

They were up in that tree house for hours before the dark and dirty secrets began to spill out. Cameron confessed about life on the edge with his junkie mom. Brandon talked without emotion about his father, who beat him regularly until the man was killed in a bar fight. His mother had disappeared long before that, so Brandon was put into the foster care system.

Adam had never known his parents. He'd been

abandoned outside a hospital at age two, then raised in an orphanage and a series of foster homes, one worse than the next. He'd been thrown out of four homes and was on a collision course with juvenile hall when Sally Duke found him and took him home.

All three boys were considered bad risks, but that hadn't deterred Sally, a young, wealthy woman who had recently lost her husband and had plenty of love to share. Sally's beloved husband had been a foster kid, too, and she wanted to give back to the system that had produced such a fine, self-made man as her husband, William.

Up in that tree house, having divulged their secrets, the three boys swore allegiance to each other. From that moment, they were blood brothers and nothing would split them apart. As part of their pact, they swore they would never get married or have kids because, based on their experience, married people hurt each other and parents hurt their kids. Even if Sally kicked them all out of her big house on the bluff overlooking Dunsmuir Bay, they swore they'd remain brothers forever.

But Sally was determined to make sure the boys knew that her home was their home, that they were a real family now. She was strict when she needed to be, but always warm and loving, and all three boys had thrived in her care. Eventually, she was able to adopt them and give them her last name. The Duke brothers grew up as a force to be reckoned with.

"Here you go," Janie announced. She placed their breakfast plates down and Adam watched his brothers begin to eat with gusto.

Adam got a coffee refill and sat back in his chair to reflect on Sally Duke, his mother, the woman who'd given three boys a chance at a good life instead of them being dragged down by a system too overburdened to care. Sally had changed the direction of their lives and made it possible for them to grow up strong and self-assured.

Adam owed her his life. But that didn't mean he would roll over and play dead just because Sally wanted to hear the pitter-patter of little rug rats around the house.

"You want some of this bacon?" Brandon asked.

"No, thanks," Adam said. He checked his watch. "I'd better run. I've got a meeting with Jerry Mansfield in half an hour."

"Wait, what are we going to do about Mom?" Brandon said.

"You worry too much," Cameron said between bites. "Nothing's going to happen."

Brandon shook his head. "We are so screwed."

"Deb, I have to go," Trish whispered. Her best friend had called to find out how the job was going but Trish couldn't concentrate, knowing Adam would be back from his meeting any minute now.

"Just one more thing," Deb said. "Ronnie's taking me out for my birthday tomorrow night."

"Do you need me to babysit?"

"No, but thanks. My mom's coming over."

"Oh, my God," Trish said as realization dawned. "Is this the first time you've been out since the baby was born?"

"Yes, and I don't know what to wear," Deb whined. "My world is elastic waistbands and maternity bras. I want to look sexy again. Help!"

Trish mentally pictured Deb's closet. She knew it as well as she knew her own. "Haven't you lost enough weight to wear your red dress?"

"Probably, except my breasts are slightly too big."

"Gee, Ronnie will hate that," Trish said drily. "Wear it."

"I really want to knock his socks off."

"Trust me," Trish said, chuckling. "He'll never know what hit him."

The floor creaked.

Trish jolted and whipped around. "Mr. Duke."

He stood several feet away by his office door. "I need the Mansfield file."

She hung up the phone. Deb would understand. Then she stood, wishing the floor could swallow her up. She couldn't believe he'd caught her on the phone. "It's on your desk, Mr. Duke."

He looked as if he were about to say something, but then he just nodded. "Good. Thanks."

"You're welcome." Trish stood rigidly, hating that she was ready to jump at his smallest command.

But he said nothing. Instead, he stared at her, then strode slowly around her area, glancing with suspicion at her desk, the files, the window. His presence was intimidating and chilling, so why did she feel as if she were burning up?

Finally, he met her gaze again. "What have you done?"

Taken aback, she said, "I—I didn't do anything."

He shook his head. "No, it looks different. You moved stuff around."

Trish relaxed her shoulders slightly and exhaled. "I didn't think you'd mind. I rearranged a few things on the desk and I moved that plant. It was blocking the view."

He raised an imperious eyebrow. "Cheryl never had time to notice the view."

"That's a shame," she said, glancing at the window. "It's gorgeous."

He stared at her intently. "Yes, it is."

Trish felt her cheeks heat up. "You don't have to worry that I'll spend all my time staring out at the ocean, Mr. Duke. I'm here to work."

"Good to know." He seemed reluctant to leave. Did he not trust her to do her work despite the tempting view of the world outside her window?

He cleared his throat, then walked toward his office. At the double doors, he turned. "Buzz me when Jerry Mansfield arrives, will you?"

"Of course, Mr. Duke," she murmured.

"And call me Adam."

"Of course."

She almost collapsed as Adam closed the door to his office. What was wrong with her? It wasn't as if she'd never seen a good-looking man before. But for some reason, this one seemed capable of mesmerizing her. As he'd stared at her, she'd felt the electric attraction. She'd been unable to breathe, aware of his every movement. She could almost feel his touch.

How was that fair? In case she'd forgotten, Adam Duke equaled the Enemy.

She rose from her desk and stood at the window where she gazed out at the wide blue expanse of ocean. What she should do is go and dunk herself in the cold water. These feelings were utterly unacceptable and she would not give in to them.

"It's just chemistry," she mumbled. She refused to feel anything but contempt for the man. After all the pain and loss she'd suffered because of him, she couldn't afford to lose her nerve now that she was so close to achieving her goal.

"So snap out of it, right now," Trish lectured herself. "What would Grandma Anna say if she could see you now?"

Trish conceded that Grandma Anna would've taken one look at Adam Duke and said, "What a hunk." Her grandmother had always had an eye for a handsome devil and her favorite line had always been, "I may be old, but I'm not dead."

But then Grandma had suffered the heart attack that led to her death. And Trish laid the blame for her grandmother's death directly at the feet of Adam Duke and his company.

If not for his cutthroat business tactics, her grandmother would still be alive and she and Trish would still live in the spacious apartment above their lovely Victorian antiques and gift shop known as Anna's Attic.

Victorian Village, the charming row of connected three-story Victorians on Sea Cove Lane, had provided homes and livelihoods for six families over several generations. Trish had grown up there, and eight months ago, right after she obtained her MBA, she'd banded together with her neighbors to look into buying the building from the long-time landlord and applying for historic landmark designation. Then everything changed. The landlord died, and before the historic landmark paperwork could go through, a development company swept in with a better bid. The landlord's children had no sentimental attachment to Victorian Village so they sold it to the highest bidder. The development company bought the block-long building, threw out the occupants and demolished their homes and livelihoods in order to build a concrete parking structure.

That company was Duke Development International.

It seemed that Adam Duke needed more parking for his expanding company, so with one sweep of his powerful hand, he had single-handedly destroyed six families' dreams. Grandma Anna's heart had literally broken after she was forced to move from the only home and business she'd known and loved since she first married her husband all those years ago.

Trish shook away the unhappy memories and hurried back to her desk. It wouldn't do to be caught staring out the window, the very thing she'd sworn not to do.

The memories helped strengthen her resolve and she went to work. On her short breaks, she pored through more files, looking for something, anything, that would connect Adam Duke to the unsavory business dealings she knew he was involved in. So far, all she'd found were neatly organized files with legitimate documentation and clearly itemized fees and costs. No double billing, no questionable investments, no shady transactions. But she knew it was only a matter of time until she found something. The destruction of her home and livelihood couldn't have been the only underhanded deal he'd negotiated in all his years in business. She knew what Adam had done probably wasn't illegal per se, but it was sneaky and unfair and mean-spirited. And she would find something eventually, some kind of evidence that would expose him as the sleazy businessman she knew he was. Only then would she fulfill the promise she'd made at her grandmother's deathbed, finally put her memories to rest and go on with her life.

By the end of the day, Trish was no closer to finding anything she might use against Adam Duke than she had been that morning. She turned off her computer and grabbed her purse, then knocked on Adam's office door. When he called out, she poked her head inside. "If there's nothing else you need, I'll be leaving for the day."

"Dammit," he muttered.

With some alarm, she checked her watch. It was almost six o'clock. "My usual hours are nine to five-thirty but I'll be glad to stay later if you need me."

"What?" Adam looked up and frowned as if just noticing her. "Oh. Sorry. You're leaving? That's fine. Have a good evening."

"What's wrong?"

He paged through the file, his mouth set in a grim line. "Something's missing from this file."

Trish's eyes widened. "I—I put everything on your desk."

"I'm sure you did." He thumbed through both stacks of papers clipped into the file. "But there's a lease amendment missing. It's got to be somewhere in the files, or maybe it's around Cheryl's—er—your desk."

"I'll check." In a panic, she rushed back to her area and rifled through the desk drawers. Had she subconsciously sabotaged a file? Of course she hadn't. She stopped and took a deep breath. Tried to relax. Then she carefully checked the file drawer, nearest to the place she'd first found the Mansfield documents.

"I think I found it," she said, walking back into Adam's office.

He jumped up from his desk and met her halfway. "Where was it?" he demanded.

"It was tucked inside the Manning file."

He rolled his eyes. "Manning. Great. I suppose that's close to Mansfield."

"Next file over."

"Good to know." He walked back to his desk where papers were scattered everywhere. "Thanks for finding this. It would've been disastrous if the client found out we'd lost it."

"I'm glad I could help."

"I just wonder how many more mistakes like this one are waiting to be found."

"I can start checking through the files tomorrow if you'd like."

"Good idea." He rubbed his knuckles across his jaw. "I guess Cheryl was under more pressure than she let on. This never would've happened if she was on top of her game."

"Three months' pregnant and trying to plan a wedding?" Trish said. "I'd call that pressure."

Adam chuckled ruefully. "Yeah, yeah. I guess I didn't help much. Still, this could've been a costly mistake. I'd appreciate it if you'd start going through the files more closely tomorrow."

"Of course." Trish almost laughed out loud at the request. She now had a legitimate reason to pore through the files and he'd handed it to her on a silver platter. She almost felt guilty, but refused to let herself go there. "Do you need anything else tonight?"

"No, thanks," Adam said as he sat back down at his desk. "You go and enjoy your evening."

She watched as he rolled his sleeves up his muscular arms. He'd long ago removed his jacket and his tie was off now. His usually well-groomed thick, dark hair was unruly and looked as if he'd combed it with his fingers more than once that afternoon.

A shiver ran up her back that had nothing to do with any temperature shift and everything to do with the ruggedly handsome man sitting before her.

She realized that she was staring. Flustered, she said, "You're working late tonight?"

"It's not that late."

She checked her watch. "It's after six."

He shrugged. "That's not late. I'll be here another few hours getting these documents finished for another meeting tomorrow."

"I can stay if you need help."

He glanced at the work spread out on his desk, then looked at her. "You don't have to."

"At least let me order you dinner before I leave."

"Not necessary."

But it was necessary. She would feel guilty all night long if she left him working alone without food. "It's not a problem."

"Well, if you're sure," he said, then pulled his wallet out and handed her a $50 bill. "That would be great. Thanks. I think Cheryl's got Angelo's Pizza on speed dial."

"Pizza? Are you sure?"

"I always order pizza when I work late."

Trish's eyes narrowed. "How often do you work late?"

"Almost every night."

"You eat pizza every night?"

He calculated, then shrugged. "Just about."

"That's not very healthy."

He grinned. "It's got all the food groups."

She simply shook her head and walked out to her desk where she found the file folder of local restaurant menus she'd seen earlier. She placed an order with a nearby restaurant for grilled chicken and rice with green beans and a salad.

She busied herself by starting on the filing project,

going through each of the folders more closely, as he'd requested. It also gave her the chance to continue her search for something incriminating, but so far, there was nothing.

After forty minutes, the food delivery arrived. She found a tray in the kitchen down the hall, laid the food out and took it into his office.

He did a double-take when she placed the tray on his desk. "What's this?"

"It's real food," she said.

He grinned. "You're pretty bossy, aren't you?"

"I just believe in good nutrition," she said defensively, and waited while he tasted everything.

He watched her with amusement as he took the first bite of chicken. "It's good."

She nodded. "And good for you."

He took another bite. "No, it's really good."

"I'm glad." She sat on the edge of the chair in front of his desk. "It'll keep you going better than pizza will."

"You may be right." After a few more bites, he said, "Marjorie mentioned you have an MBA."

"You were listening?"

His lips twisted in a self-deprecating grin. "Okay, fine, I deserved that."

Her eyes widened. "Oh, I didn't mean—"

"It's okay," he said with a laugh. "But in my own defense, I've had to deal with some of our floaters before. You haven't."

"Did you mean special assignment assistants?" Trish said, biting back a smile.

He laughed again. "Okay, I was an ass."

She couldn't help but laugh. "I wouldn't say that."

"You didn't have to say it," he said wryly.

"But you had a right to be angry," Trish allowed. "I

can't imagine someone leaving you high and dry in the middle of such an important deal."

He bit into a green bean. "I'm still angry. But I suppose I'm somewhat to blame. Cheryl did mention getting married a few times, but I've been so wrapped up in the Fantasy Mountain deal, I guess I let it go in one ear and out the other."

"This is the ski resort I've heard so much about?" She'd seen the photographs of the resort lining the walls of the lobby downstairs.

"Yeah," Adam said, taking another bite of chicken. "We're closing the deal at the end of the month and we've planned a major celebration. The investors and their families will be staying there for a long weekend. There'll be a big formal party and lots of hoopla. If we can get our act together."

"I'm sure it'll come together nicely," Trish said. "The photos of the resort look beautiful."

He sat forward in his chair. "It's a great place, Trish. Top-of-the-line luxury, with a spa and a world-class restaurant, great trails and ski runs. It's fabulous. The rooms are rustic, but warm and beautiful and elegant at the same time. I can't wait to show it off."

Trish couldn't help but get caught up in his enthusiasm. "It sounds wonderful."

Adam looked thoughtful. "Cheryl was in charge of the big opening-night gala we're throwing for the investors."

"A gala?"

"Red carpet, formal ball, the whole bit."

"Sounds exciting."

He stabbed at a small piece of chicken. "It will be if we can still pull it off. That's something else I'll need to bring you up to speed on tomorrow."

"Oh, I'd love to work on something like that. I've always dreamed—" She stopped. Whoa. No dreaming, please. What was she thinking? She'd been drawn in by his charm again. She carefully checked her watch, then stood. "Naturally, I'll be glad to do whatever you need me to do. I'd better be going now. I'll see you in the morning."

Adam seemed surprised by her abrupt change in attitude, but said smoothly, "Of course, it's late. Thanks again for everything. See you tomorrow."

"Yes, good night." She hurried out of his office, grabbed her purse off her desktop and raced to the elevator. As she waited, she berated herself. What was wrong with her, sitting around chatting with him as though they were the best of friends? Lest she forget, Adam Duke was not her friend and never would be.

And furthermore, as far as the opening-night gala was concerned, if she managed to complete the *real* job she'd come here to do, she'd be long gone before the Fantasy Mountain formal ball ever took place.

Three

She should've quit yesterday.

It was now Trish's fourth day on the job. She'd been through every file drawer along one long wall of her workspace but had found absolutely nothing incriminating about Adam Duke. Nothing that could be used to create even the tiniest public outcry against him and his company. On the contrary, yesterday she'd stumbled upon a full drawer of files containing the many charitable foundations he served on, along with pages and pages of donations he'd given over the years. The man seemed to be a veritable paragon.

"He even wants to save the whales," she muttered.

But that's not why she should've quit. She wanted whales to have a good life, too. And it was great that he supported all those charities. But did Adam have to come across as such a Boy Scout? She knew he wasn't, knew all those good deeds were just a façade to cover up the slimier projects his company carried out. There were plenty more files to search and she knew she'd find something eventually. She had to. She'd been here almost a week and so far he'd treated her so nicely, she was racked with guilt.

But that wasn't the reason why she should've quit, either. No, the reason was that she was starting to *like* Adam Duke. And not just because he was beyond handsome, not just because her heart stammered whenever he got close to her and not just because she was starting to dream of him at night. God help her.

No. The problem was, she was starting to like *him*. The man himself. His sense of humor, his sense of right and wrong, his work ethic, the way he treated his subordinates. Everyone in the company seemed to adore him and as much as she'd fought it, she found herself teetering dangerously close to that slippery slope. And adoration was not, repeat, *not* listed on her business plan.

And even if she did adore him—which she *didn't*—Adam Duke was the last person on earth she would ever get involved with. Not that he'd asked her out or anything. He never would. She was his employee and he was probably too damn conscientious to ever cross that line. And that was fine, too. She'd heard enough office gossip to know that she wasn't his type at all. Meaning, she wasn't a supermodel, tall and thin and beautiful—if vapid. Nor was she the type to fall into bed with a man just because he took her out to dinner.

She fumed as she slammed shut another file drawer. Even if he did ask her out to that fancy dinner, she would say no. Because Adam Duke was the enemy.

"Remember, Trish?" she muttered fiercely under her

breath. "That's why you're here. The man is the *enemy*. Try to stay on track, would you?"

"Good morning, Trish," Adam said.

Okay, she might've let out the eensiest little squeal, but she applauded herself for not jumping more than six inches at the sound of his voice. Why did he continue to sneak up on her?

"Good morning," she whispered hoarsely, trying to catch her breath.

"You're trying to make me look bad, aren't you?" he said, gazing at her through narrowed eyes.

"What? Me? No." She glanced around quickly. The file drawers were closed. There were no incriminating notes on her desk. How had he grasped the true reason why she was here?

He laughed and every last synapse in her nervous system stood up and did the cha-cha-cha. Who needed coffee when Adam Duke was in the room?

She cleared her throat and moved to her desk. "I'm not sure what you mean."

"I thought I'd be the first one in the office," he explained. "But you've beat me to it every day this week and here you are again, already settled in and hard at work."

"Oh." She was such a moron. "Right." She tried to breathe evenly as she fiddled with the staple remover and almost gouged her thumb. "Um, well, I do like to get an early start on things."

"Great," he said with a wink and a crooked smile. "I like that, too."

She resisted the urge to check her pulse. She looked away, tried to swallow, but her throat was dry as dust.

"Everything okay this morning?" Adam asked.

"Uh, yes."

"Any calls?"

"No, sir."

"Sir?" He grinned. "I like the sound of that."

She shook her head. There was that teasing sense of humor again. And that, combined with a winning smile, was surely the most attractive quality in any man. Well, a perfectly shaped rear end helped, and Adam Duke had that going for him, too.

"Are you ready to go over the opening-night arrangements?" she asked as Adam turned toward his office.

"Absolutely," he said. "Grab your notes and come in."

Trish squelched the thought that her notepad wasn't the only thing she wanted to grab. As she followed him into his office, she took it all in: the perfect butt, the wide shoulders, his masculine scent, his powerful stride. The man exuded strength, charisma and incredible sex appeal, and his ethics had the appearance of being honorable. So what was she doing here? Besides tormenting herself, of course? Lust, forbidden and sweet, roiled inside her and she almost groaned. How could she be so stupid as to be falling for him?

She really should've quit yesterday.

Adam ignored the now-familiar tightness pulling at his groin and sat down behind the heavy mahogany desk. By now, he should've been used to this ridiculous lust and the physical manifestation it produced in him every time he walked into the office and feasted his eyes on the deliciously curvaceous Trish James.

Physical manifestation? He rolled his eyes in disgust. Why not call it a hard-on and be done with it? But hey, wouldn't his brothers be proud that he was using his words?

Despite the physical…whatever, Adam had to admit he got a kick out of seeing Trish every morning. She was adorable without even trying to be, and it was easy and fun to spook her. You'd think she was up to no good, the way she startled so easily.

His chuckle got lost somewhere in his chest as he watched her plant herself in the chair opposite him and cross her legs. She was wearing a dress today and it was just as he'd suspected: her legs were world class. Smooth, shapely and lightly tanned, they were accentuated by three-inch heels that made Adam wish they were all she was wearing. He would start at her ankles, kissing and licking his way up to—

"Before we go over my notes," Trish began, "there's a letter you should probably read." She pulled a piece of correspondence from his inbox and handed it to him. "It looks important."

Adam raised his eyebrows when he saw the law firm letterhead and was scowling by the time he finished reading the contents.

He grabbed the phone and hit the speed-dial number of the contractor on-site at Fantasy Mountain. Holding up one finger to let Trish know this wouldn't take long, he waited for his call to be put through. He and his brothers hired Bob Paxton Construction for all their projects because Bob was simply the best in the business. And the Duke brothers only worked with the best.

Ten minutes later, Adam hung up the phone.

"I take it the news is bad?" Trish asked.

He glanced over, noticed her look of concern and realized that he was grateful she was so in tune with him and his business. It felt good to have someone on his side. Almost instantly, he brushed that odd feeling away and stood to pace.

"Yeah, it's bad news," he said, walking across the room to the coffeepot. He poured himself a cup and held the pot out to Trish.

"No, thanks," she said, still wearing that look of consternation. "Did someone get hurt at Fantasy Mountain?"

"No," Adam said immediately. "You read the letter, right?"

"Yes," she said, making a face. "But the legalese made my eyes cross."

"I know what you mean." Adam chuckled and sat back down at his desk. "But I assure you, nobody was hurt."

"Then what happened? Can you discuss it?"

"Yeah. The ADA guidelines weren't followed for the parking structures." He set the coffee mug on the corner of his desk.

"ADA is the Americans with Disabilities Act?"

"Right," Adam said, impressed that Trish had heard of the federal act. He'd had to explain it more than once to Cheryl when she'd first started working for him. "We make every effort to comply with the ADA, not only because we don't want to get sued, but also, more importantly, because we want everyone to be able to enjoy the experience our resorts have to offer. It's a no-brainer. But somehow, the subcontractor who built the parking structure didn't comply with the guidelines."

"The guidelines tell you how many spaces you need for handicapped parking and that sort of thing?"

"Right," Adam said, pleased once again that she was aware of the issues involved. "It's a lot more complicated than that, though, right down to the angles of curbs and degrees of slope, the width of sidewalks, the height of sinks in the bathrooms. I could bore you to tears with all the details. But the bottom line is, the crew building the parking lot screwed up."

"How did this lawyer find out about it?" she asked, pointing to the letter.

"Good question," Adam said, taking another sip of coffee. "There are organizations that make it their business to check out new facilities like hotels, shopping centers, public spaces, to make sure that the ADA guidelines are followed to the letter. That way, they can assure their members that they'll have access to all areas."

"That's probably a good idea."

"Yes, it is," he said, and ordinarily he had no trouble with the inspections. Because the Dukes had never had a problem. Until now. "So now we've got to get it fixed before the resort opens."

"Can it be done that fast?"

"That's what the phone call was for. Bob's already on it. In fact, he's more furious than I am. He'll get the subcontractor back there to clean up their mess. I want them to start as soon as possible, but before anything can happen, this lawyer wants to survey the site with us and point out everything that's wrong."

She gave him an understanding smile. "You don't like lawyers."

"They're a necessary evil," Adam said, shrugging. Then he grinned. "Besides, my lawyers can beat up anyone else's lawyers any day."

Trish laughed. "I'm sure they can."

As pleased as he was to have made Trish laugh, he quickly sobered. "I don't want to make light of this situation. I grew up with plenty of handicapped kids in the orphanage, so I know the problems they face."

Whoa, where had that come from?

He rushed to change the subject even as Trish's eyes

widened in sympathy. "So while this problem is stupid and annoying, it's not irreparable."

She nodded slowly, but didn't say anything, and Adam knew that if he could've kicked himself, he would have. He'd never made a slip like that before. What was he doing, talking about the orphanage to someone outside of his own family? It was none of the world's business what his life had been like before Sally Duke had intervened. Sure, reporters had dug out the truth in the past, but he preferred never to discuss it at all.

"We'll need the jet," he said abruptly.

She blinked. "We have a jet?"

He simply nodded, then punched up his calendar on the computer. "Yeah, we've got a jet. I'll need you to call and book it for Wednesday morning."

She snapped back into business mode and began writing in her notepad. "Wednesday morning. Where and when?"

"Let's make it eight o'clock. Leaving Dunsmuir Airport and traveling to the Fantasy Mountain airstrip. They've made the flight before. Let them know what you want for breakfast, and tell them I'll have the usual."

She looked up, mystified. "The usual? Wait. Breakfast? Me? Why?"

He grinned as she tripped over her words. "Breakfast is the most important meal of the day."

She shook her head in exasperation. "You don't need me to go with you."

"Of course I do," he said, breezing over her protest. He strolled to the wet bar, placed the coffee mug in the little sink, then casually added, "And pack an overnight bag."

"What?" She jumped up from the chair and blocked his way back to his desk. "Why?"

He gazed into her beautiful, leaf-green eyes and almost forgot what they were talking about. Almost. "It might be a long day. We could get stuck on the mountain. You never know about the weather in November." He could hear the tension in his own voice and wondered why a discussion of travel arrangements made him feel as horny as a high school kid.

"I suppose," she said slowly, but she didn't look at all convinced. She obviously didn't want to go to Fantasy Mountain, but the more she protested, the more he wanted her with him. She was so close, he itched to take her in his arms and fuse her body to his. But that probably wouldn't help his cause just now.

"Besides bringing you up to speed on the ADA issues," he explained, "this'll be a good time for you to take a look at the space for the opening-night festivities."

"Really, Adam, I don't see why..." Her shoulders slumped and she blew out a breath.

Adam stared at her for a moment. "Trish, are you afraid of flying?"

"Of course not," she said indignantly, her chin held high.

"Good. Be ready to leave at eight o'clock Wednesday morning."

"Fine."

He sat down at his desk again and said, "We'll go over your notes for the opening-night festivities while we're in the air next week. I won't have time to do it until then. And right now, I need you to pull some files."

Once Trish left the office, Adam could breathe again.

Pensively, he stood up, strolled to the wide bank of windows and stared out at the coast. He'd been walking an increasingly narrow tightrope over the last few days, trying to keep his mind on business despite being barraged by sexual fantasies that featured his attractive new assistant.

"Dammit." He couldn't blame Trish. She was efficient, discreet and intelligent. She seemed to have a good sense of humor. Adam noticed he'd been laughing a lot more lately and wondered if too much laughter was rotting his brain.

The woman was not only good at her job, but actually seemed to care about him. Hell, she even made sure he ordered something healthy for dinner every night he worked late. She'd stood her ground on the health food issue again last night and he'd admired her style while at the same time he'd debated whether he could rip off her clothes, throw her onto his couch and satisfy his true hunger.

Adam had already identified the problem. Lust. Pure and simple. He knew it. He just didn't know what to do about it. Well, no, actually, he knew exactly what to do about it, he thought ruefully. He just couldn't figure out when he would have a free minute to find a willing woman and satisfy that particular itch until the Fantasy Mountain resort was a done deal.

He wasn't going to give in to what he felt for Trish. Not while she was working for him.

So it promised to be one hell of a frustrating month.

An hour later, the intercom rang and Adam grabbed the phone. "What?" he asked a little too curtly.

"It's your brother Brandon on line 2," Trish announced.

"Thanks."

Adam pushed the speakerphone button. "What's up?"

"Who was that?" Brandon asked immediately.

"My new assistant."

"Is she hot?"

"I'm hanging up now."

"She must be hot."

"Goodbye, Brandon."

"Wait," Brandon said quickly. "Just wanted to alert you to the fact that Mom had dinner with Marjorie last night."

"So what?"

"Don't you get it?" Brandon demanded. "Marjorie's one of Mom's oldest friends. She's got to be in on the scheme. Think about it. Mom's got our own Human Resources manager working to sabotage us from within the company. They're perfectly positioned to bring you down."

"You're nuts."

"Fine. But don't say I didn't warn you. Mom's turned desperate and ruthless. I actually heard her say that you're going down first, so you'd better be on your guard. Don't be surprised if they pull an inside job."

Adam shook his head as his brother's ranting came to an end. "When did you become so paranoid?"

"Call me names but heed my words," Brandon said in a serious tone, then added, "Mom wants grandkids and to get what she wants, she has to sacrifice us. You're her first target, so I'm just saying you might want to beware of strange and beautiful women running amok in your office."

Adam laughed. "Were you hit in the head with one too many footballs?"

"This is the thanks I get for watching your back?"

"Talk to you later, bro," Adam said, shaking his head.

"I can only hope so," Brandon said mournfully, then quickly reminded him about the weekend barbecue at their mother's house.

Adam was still chuckling when he hung up. He buzzed Trish and asked her to bring him the North Vineyard file. She entered his office and his gaze was immediately drawn to her legs. Again. The dress she wore was office appropriate. Almost too conservative, in fact. It shouldn't have been sexy, so why were his nerves humming as he watched how well the silky material clung to her curves and skimmed her knees as she made her way across the room?

Small silver buttons ran up the front of Trish's dress and Adam wondered how long it would take to unbutton them enough to allow the soft fabric to slide off her shoulders and reveal her enticing breasts. In no time, he would have her naked, under him, on his desk.

"Do you want it on your desk?" she asked.

Adam flinched. Could she read his mind? He looked up to see her smiling as she held the thick client folder out for him to take. He exhaled heavily. Chances were, she wouldn't be smiling if she knew which direction his mind drifted off to whenever she walked into the office.

"Adam?"

"Yeah." What the hell was wrong with him? He felt a headache brewing and pinched the bridge of his nose. "On the desk. Thanks, Trish."

"I didn't know your company owned vineyards."

"What?"

She pointed to the file. "North Vineyard is part of Duke Cellars. I never made the connection until now."

"Oh." He rubbed his forehead and tried to concentrate on the mundane topic. "Yes. We own a number of vineyards and we've just had our fourth press. It promises to be a good one. We'll be opening a resort in the wine country next year."

"Oh, that sounds exciting."

"Yeah, it should be a fantastic opening."

Her eyes glittered with interest and all he could think about was making them shine with passion.

"Are you all right?" she asked, concern in her voice.

"Oh, yeah, great," he said, clamping down on his urge to pull her onto his lap.

"Are you sure I can't do anything for you?"

Not unless she was willing to give him a full body massage. "Thanks, no. I'll be fine."

She didn't look convinced. "Okay, but I'm right outside and I have aspirin if you need it."

A cold shower would be more of a help, but Adam nodded. "I appreciate it."

She turned to leave and he caught the lightest scent of oranges and vanilla. Against his better judgment, he savored the sweetness as he watched her long-legged gait carry her across the thickly carpeted office toward the door. The sway of her curvaceous bottom hypnotized him completely.

Dammit, would he ever be able to relax in his own office again?

Beware of strange and beautiful women running amok in your office.

"What the—?" He looked around, then made a face as Brandon's words managed to filter through his distracted mind.

Trish turned. "Did you say something?"

"No," he said in a strangled tone he barely recognized as his own.

"Okay." She smiled, then slipped out and quietly shut the door behind her.

An inside job.

"Stop it," he said aloud, shaking his head in protest. Brandon was seriously deranged and Adam was buying into his obsession, that was all.

You're her first target.

"No, I'm not."

She's ruthless and desperate.

"There's no way." He shook his head again and cursed under his breath, then brusquely opened the North Vineyard file and started to study the lease terms. After reading the same convoluted sentence three times, he stopped, looked up and stared at the closed doors leading to Trish's work area.

They're perfectly positioned to bring you down.

He raked his fingers through his hair as he recalled Marjorie's words four days ago, the morning she brought Trish in to take Cheryl's place as his assistant.

I've got the perfect person for you, Marjorie had said. And she'd been damn cheery about it, too.

"Ah, hell," he muttered. There was no way his brother Brandon was right. It was ludicrous. Trish? A plant? A willing player in his mother's scheme to marry him off?

Or was she just a pawn?

Adam pushed away from his desk and began to pace. He stopped. Shook his head. Paced some more. Stopped again.

He was driving himself crazy.

How could his mother and Marjorie pull off something like this? First of all, they would've had to have orchestrated Cheryl's departure. Or would they? Maybe it was just a happy coincidence that Cheryl had left the company, and Marjorie, coerced by his mother, had jumped at the opportunity to bring in a certain attractive woman who just might be capable of seducing him into love and marriage.

His eyes narrowed as he conjured up a picture of Mom and Marjorie meeting, scheming, conniving to pull it off.

Suddenly, it didn't seem at all far-fetched.

Abruptly, he remembered Trish's own words, the ones he'd overheard her say to someone on the phone the other day.

Trust me, he won't know what hit him.

Had Trish been talking to his mother? Or Marjorie, perhaps? It was obvious from her words that something shady was going on.

Did he really need more proof than that?

No. He had all the ammunition he needed.

He had to hand it to them, he admitted with a short laugh. Nice try. Trish was definitely attractive, and while he might enjoy the seduction part, there was no way in hell he'd fall for the whole love-and-marriage package.

He stared out the window at the waves crashing against the cliffs south of Dunsmuir Bay. He and his brothers had bought this land and built their company in this spot specifically to take advantage of the view. Despite the advantages Sally Duke had given them, they'd worked their asses off to get their company to the place it was today. He wouldn't allow some gold digger to get her greedy paws on half of all that.

Raking a frustrated hand through his hair, he turned from the window and grabbed a bottle of water from the sideboard. It just figured that Mom would pick out someone smart and nurturing like Trish to be his mate. Yes, she was beautiful, too, but her beauty was fresh and healthy, nothing like the calculated, sophisticated, worldly women he'd always dated in the past. He knew his mother disapproved of those types of women, but they filled the bill as far as Adam was concerned. Women who wanted no strings, no obligations, just healthy, raucous sex when the spirit moved them. Nothing wrong with that.

He suddenly recalled his mother's face as he'd introduced her to one of those women at a charity ball they'd both attended a few weeks earlier. At the time, he thought he'd read disappointment in the way Mom stared at him, the way her lips were pursed and her jaw was set. But it wasn't disappointment at all, Adam realized now. It was determination. He'd seen a new sense of purpose in his mother's eyes that night.

Determination to marry him off at the earliest possible date.

Adam rubbed his jaw, unsure of his next move. It was beginning to sink in, what Brandon had been dealing with since he'd temporarily moved back in with their mother. Sally Duke was a force of nature and it would be dangerous to underestimate her.

The more Adam pondered the odds that Trish had been planted here by his mother and Marjorie, the more plausible the whole thing seemed. The only question that remained was whether Trish was aware of their scheme. If she was in on the plan, and landing a rich husband like Adam was the only reason she was working here, then that made her a gold digger—plain and simple. An attractive gold digger, to be sure. But that meant she was fair game and ripe for outmaneuvering.

Pacing the length of his office and back, Adam mused over the possibilities. Trish James was perfect, absolutely perfect. Not for him, certainly, but for Mom's imaginary view of what a prospective wife for her son should be like.

And the more he thought about it, the more he had to admit how impressed he was. His mother had almost pulled one over on him.

"Well played, Mom," Adam murmured with a calculated grin. "And don't worry, there'll be a seduction, all right."

He'd seduce the lovely gold digger, enjoy a few nights of hot, delicious sex, then send her on her way.

"But not right away," he murmured as the plan took shape in his mind. After all, he had Fantasy Mountain to consider, and Trish was doing a great job organizing everything that would make the opening gala an event that would be talked about for years to come. Once it was over, though, he would kiss Trish James goodbye. Literally. He'd send the gold digger packing while also sending a clear message to his meddling mother that he would not tolerate her interfering in his life again.

With any luck, that would put an end to this ridiculous matchmaking scheme once and for all.

Four

"So it's as horrible as you thought it would be?"

"No, no," Trish said, keeping her voice perky. "It's going great."

It was Friday night, the end of an exhausting week. Trish tried to relax with a glass of chilled chardonnay while her best friend Deb Perris coaxed her three-month-old baby to drink milk from a bottle. They sat in Deb's comfortable family room directly across the breakfast bar from the kitchen.

"You never were a very good liar," Deb remarked.

"Why would I lie?" Trish asked.

"Gosh, I don't know." Deb brushed a few soft strands of Gavin's hair off his forehead. "Maybe you're trying to hide something. But here's a little hint. If you think raising your voice two octaves higher than normal makes you sound happy, you're wrong."

Trish leaned forward to tug at little Gavin's tiny

foot. "Poor baby, you'll never be able to get away with anything."

"That's right," Deb said proudly. "So you might as well spill the beans. Is the man as bad as you thought he would be?"

"Worse," Trish muttered before taking another hearty sip of wine to dull the misery.

"Really? Worse? How thrilling." Deb pulled the bottle out of Gavin's mouth to check how much milk was left. The baby began to fuss.

"Don't worry, sweetie," she crooned. "There's plenty more." She popped the bottle back into his mouth, then looked at Trish, unable to hide her excitement. "You know, I'm not surprised. Everyone at DDI seems to love him, but it's always a different story when you get them behind closed doors. Figures the richest ones are always the biggest jerks."

"But that's the problem," Trish grumbled. "The big jerk isn't turning out to be quite the jerk we thought he'd be. Just the opposite, in fact. He's thoughtful and funny and a true Good Samaritan—if all those charity files are to be believed. You should've seen how angry he got when he found out the contractors messed things up for handicapped guests at the resort."

"You're kidding," Deb said. "He sounds like some kind of white knight."

"I know." Trish took another healthy gulp of wine. She wasn't about to mention the orphanage Adam had spent time in. Not that she cared about his sensibilities. But good grief, how was she supposed to deal with the man she'd declared her sworn enemy when, despite what he'd done to her home and her family, she was actually starting to like him?

"Huh," Deb said. "There's got to be *something* wrong with him."

"Not so far," Trish griped.

"Oh, come on," Deb persisted. "I can tell you're holding out on me and that's not fair. I'm stuck here blathering baby talk all day, every day. So throw me a bone, would you? A little gossip? Something? Anything?"

Trish laughed. "I've got nothing."

"I'm not above begging," Deb said as she fiddled with the baby's blanket. "I don't get out much. And not that it's an issue or anything, but let's face it, you owe me."

"Hey, I steered you toward wearing the red dress, didn't I?"

"Not good enough," Deb said, laughing. "Although Ronnie was a happy man. Come on, spill."

Trish sighed. It's true that if it weren't for Deb, she might never have been hired by Duke Development International in the first place. When Deb left her administrative job at DDI to stay home with the baby, she'd recommended Trish to Marjorie Wallace, the HR manager, who'd immediately hired Trish for the special assignment department. Trish never would've been able to infiltrate the company so quickly if not for Deb. So, yes, she owed her friend the truth—if only she could figure out exactly what the truth was.

"You could've warned me how dangerous this job could be to my health," she groused, getting up to pour herself another half glass of the delicious crisp, dry wine. As she pushed the cork back into the bottle and returned it to the refrigerator shelf, she noticed the label. *Duke Cellars.* Oh, great. She couldn't escape the man for one minute.

Deb gave her a quizzical look. "What do you mean, dangerous?"

Trish waved a hand to negate her words. "It's nothing."

Deb persisted. "Hey, if there's a problem, you don't have to handle it alone. You could—"

"It's just—" Trish exhaled heavily. "It's hard to breathe when he's standing by my desk."

Her friend's smile was smug. "He really is cute, isn't he?"

"Cute?" Trish repeated, stunned by the word. When had Deb become such a master of understatement? *Cute* was for puppy dogs and two-year-olds. *Devastating* would more accurately describe Adam Duke.

"But as I recall," Deb continued, "I *did* warn you. You just weren't ready to listen. You were on a mission, remember?"

Trish sipped her wine. "I still am."

"You still intend to go through with it?"

"I have to."

Deb shrugged, put the now-empty baby bottle on the side table, then lifted the baby to her shoulder. After a few pats, Gavin let out a healthy burp and they both laughed.

"What a good boy," Deb whispered, bouncing the baby lightly in her arms.

Trish couldn't prevent the pang of envy that tripped up her heart as she watched. Deb and she had been best friends since fourth grade when Deb's parents moved their family to Dunsmuir Bay. Two years ago, Trish had been maid of honor when Deb married her high school sweetheart, Ronnie, in a beautiful ceremony on the cliff overlooking the bay. Then little Gavin was born three months ago and Deb quit her job to stay home.

Trish smiled wistfully. She didn't really envy her friend's happiness, but sometimes she wished things had turned out differently in her own life. If Grandma were still alive, if Anna's Attic and the Victorian Village were still standing, her life might've taken another road, might've turned out more like Deb's. She might have a husband or even a baby of her own by now.

Resolve trickled through her as she reminded herself that whatever else he appeared to be, Adam Duke was the reason her world had fallen to pieces. And Trish wasn't the only one who'd been affected. There were others depending on her to keep her word to bring Adam down. If she ever wanted to face her old friends and neighbors again, she needed to be strong and follow through on her plan.

Maybe someday, when Adam Duke and his machinations had been dealt with and were a thing of the past, she might think about settling down. But not yet. Not until she could look herself in the mirror and feel some amount of pride at having fulfilled the promise she'd made to Grandma Anna on her deathbed.

Content that little Gavin was settled and happy in his infant seat, Deb sat back down. "I know this plan of yours is something you've thought about for a long time, but if you've had a change of heart, it's okay. You're free to change your mind anytime you want."

"I won't change my mind," Trish said.

"There's no shame in it," Deb insisted. "You've got an accounting degree and an MBA. You could get a job anywhere."

"I know, and I will," she said, gazing at her friend with renewed resolve. "But first things first. My personal feelings about Adam Duke don't matter. He deserves to be taken down and I won't give up until I've done just that."

* * *

Trish spent most of Saturday morning running errands. She stopped at the dry cleaners, the grocery store, the bank and finally the library where she returned two books, then strolled over to browse the new arrivals shelf.

"My goodness, is that you, Trish?"

She turned, then smiled and gave the chic, older woman a hug. "Mrs. Collins, how are you?"

"I'm as well as can be expected for an old gal." Selma Collins was a neighbor from Victorian Village. She'd owned the stylish clothing shop that had provided Trish with dresses for all the significant events of her life, from her first communion to her senior prom.

Today Mrs. Collins wore one of her vintage Chanel suits. It was almost as old as she was, but it was elegant and timeless, just as she was. Her subtle scent of Chanel No. 5 filled Trish's sense memory and, just for a moment, transported her back to a happier time.

"Oh, Mrs. Collins," Trish said with a grin, "you look as fresh and young as the day I met you."

The woman slapped Trish's arm. "My dear, you were a toddler when I first met you, so stop pulling this old gal's leg."

They both chuckled, then Trish wasn't sure what to say. Most of the neighbors knew her plan to infiltrate Duke Development and they'd applauded her for taking action. But if she came up with nothing, she didn't know how she would face them. And that outcome was looking more and more inevitable with every day she spent with Adam Duke.

"You probably heard that Claude and Madeleine had to declare bankruptcy," Mrs. Collins whispered.

The news hit Trish like a physical blow to the chest.

Claude and Madeleine Maubert had operated the Village Patisserie for over twenty years. Their chocolate croissants were the stuff of dreams. Trish had loved hearing Mrs. Maubert's stories of her life in Paris before she met her husband and they ventured "across the pond," as she always said. "Oh, no. Are they going to be all right?"

Mrs. Collins shook her head. "They went through most of their savings trying to set up another patisserie like the one they'd had at the Village, but they just couldn't make it work. I don't think their hearts were in it."

"I wish there was something I could do to help."

"Oh, dear girl, you're doing everything you can." Mrs. Collins squeezed her arm. "We have such great hopes for you."

Trish smiled thinly but said nothing. She wished now that she hadn't raised the expectations of her neighbors by telling them of her plan to find some dirt on Adam Duke. Even if she did discover something they could use against their nemesis, it wouldn't bring back their shops or their homes.

But eight months ago, after Grandma Anna died, Trish had been so angry and hurt that she'd stormed into City Hall and demanded to know why the city hadn't approved the historical designation for Victorian Village. They'd told her that renters couldn't apply for the designation; it had to come from the owners.

She remembered the overwhelming desire to throw something at the clerk. It shouldn't have mattered who applied for the designation. It was an objective fact that the block-long building was a town landmark, well over one hundred years old and lovingly preserved in the classic Queen Anne Victorian style. How dare the city allow it to be bulldozed into oblivion and replaced by a concrete slab?

After receiving no satisfaction at City Hall, she'd marched into the large Duke Development construction trailer that was camped on the site of her razed home and made silly threats. The head guy, a wormy little man who made her skin crawl, had warned her to get out or he would call security, so she left of her own accord, but not before foolishly ranting her intention to "take down Duke Development" if it was the last thing she did.

Now, she could only laugh ruefully at the memory but back then, she'd been carrying around a grudge that weighed her down like a stone. Soon after the embarrassing scene at the Duke construction trailer, Trish had attended a barbecue with her old neighbors. She'd shared her plan with them, boldly promising that she would find something—anything—that could be used to hurt the Dukes in some way. It had been rash of her, but her friends had hailed her as their heroine and bolstered her confidence, so she knew she had to give it her best shot.

And so she had. But so far, she'd found nothing remotely damaging to the corporation or to Adam Duke himself. On the contrary, the man appeared to be a saint.

Mrs. Collins hugged her again and told her to "keep the fight alive." Trish promised to arrange a get-together soon, then watched the older woman walk away. Trish knew she had no choice but to renew her pledge to continue her search. She just prayed that Adam never found out her true intentions because, if he did, she had no doubt that he would make it impossible for her to ever find work in this town again.

* * *

"Who wants hot dogs?" Sally Duke cried as she slid the patio door open while balancing two full platters of hot dogs and buns.

"Let me help you with that, Mom," Adam said, jogging over to grab something from her capable hands. He set the trays on the patio table.

"Thanks, sweetie," Sally said. "Could you make the hamburger patties? You're so good at that."

"I'll take care of them. You relax."

"Oh, and I think we'll need more sangria."

"You got it." Adam signaled to Brandon, who stood behind the tiki bar on the other side of the wide terrace, beyond the pool. "Mom needs more sangria."

"Coming right up," Brandon called.

Adam entered the big, sunny kitchen where Cameron stood at the stove, putting the finishing touches on the latest batch of his world-famous chili.

Adam snatched a pickle from the relish tray in the refrigerator and chomped it down before heading over to taste-test the chili.

"Needs salt," he said after the first spoonful.

"I know," Cameron said.

Adam pulled the hamburger meat from the refrigerator, grabbed a large glass bowl from the cupboard and cleared a spot on the kitchen island to work.

"I need to talk to you and Brandon some time today," Cameron said as he stirred the pot. "The environmental report came in on the Monarch Beach property and I want to take action on Monday."

"Sounds good," Adam said. "I've got an ADA issue going on at Fantasy Mountain, too."

"Speaking of fantasies," Brandon said as he walked

into the room carrying the empty sangria pitcher. "How's that sweet new assistant of yours doing?"

Cameron turned. "You've got a new assistant?"

"Mind your own damn business," Adam said gruffly to Brandon.

"Ouch," Brandon said, grinning as he ladled more sangria from the punch bowl into the pitcher. "I seem to have touched a nerve."

He left the kitchen to deliver the sangria but was back in less than a minute. "What did I miss?"

"I believe we were about to discuss Adam's new assistant," Cameron said drily.

Dammit, this subject wasn't going to go away. Might as well discuss it with people he trusted. Adam walked to the sink and pulled the kitchen curtain back in order to scan the patio. "Where's Mom?"

"Marjorie and Bea just arrived," Brandon said. "They're all out at the bar, drinking sangria and wolfing down chips and salsa."

"Good," Adam said, suddenly feeling almost as paranoid as Brandon had earlier in the week. "Let's make sure they stay out there."

"What's going on?" Cameron asked. "You don't want Mom to know about this ADA issue?"

Brandon snickered as he grabbed a beer from the refrigerator. "I'm betting he's not really worried about the ADA issue right now."

"Shut up," Adam grumbled as he kneaded garlic powder into the meat.

"He hates when I'm right," Brandon said, smirking.

"Luckily, that rarely happens," Adam said drily.

"Good one," Brandon said, too amused to counter the jibe. "So go ahead, just spill it."

It wasn't that easy, Adam thought, staring at his

brothers. They'd always shared their problems with each other. Despite Brandon's easygoing nature, he had instincts as sharply drawn as Adam's and Cameron's. Besides being his brothers, these two men were his business partners and the two people he most trusted with his life. So he took a breath and spilled his guts.

"It's this thing Brandon's been harping on," he said, glancing from Cameron to Brandon. "You know, about Mom's latest campaign."

Cameron looked puzzled for a second, then said, "The matchmaking thing?"

"Yeah."

"What about it?"

Adam hesitated, then said, "I've got this new assistant."

Brandon nodded. "She's very hot."

"You've seen her?" Cameron turned to Adam. "When did he get to see her?"

Adam rolled his eyes. "He hasn't seen her."

"No," Brandon said, "but I've talked to her on the phone. Her voice is very hot."

"So?" Cameron turned to Adam. "Is she hot or what?"

Adam shook his head as he added more seasonings to the meat. His brothers were nothing if not predictable when it came to women. "Yeah, she's hot. That's the problem."

"I don't really see that as a problem," Cameron said, grinning. "But that's just me."

Brandon chuckled, then took a sip of beer.

"Okay, I'll bite." Cameron shrugged. "So what does your hot assistant have to do with Mom and…" He stopped, stared at Adam, then Brandon, then back to Adam. "No way," he whispered in amazement.

"Way, bro," Brandon said, nodding sagely.

"She wouldn't," Cameron said. "Would she?"

"Wouldn't she?" Adam asked. "We are talking about Sally Duke, right? The woman known far and wide as the Steel Camellia?"

"Right," Brandon said, then added, "the woman everyone in town calls when they need to accomplish the impossible."

"But…how?" Cameron thought for another few seconds, then asked, "Wait a minute. You already have an assistant. Where's Cheryl?"

"She quit," Adam said flatly.

"Cheryl quit?" Cameron frowned at the chili, then glanced at Adam. "What's happening with the Fantasy Mountain opening?"

"Trish hit the ground running with that project," he said, realizing again that no matter what her reason was for being in his office, she was damn good at her job. "She's got it covered."

"Trish. Your new assistant."

"Yeah."

"So she's good."

"She's excellent."

"Where'd you find her?"

Adam paused, then admitted, "The floater pool."

Cameron whipped around. "What?"

"You didn't tell me that," Brandon said.

"I know what you're thinking."

Cameron's eyes narrowed. "I'm not sure you do."

"Does she know what she's doing?" Brandon asked.

"Completely," Adam said as he pulled a cookie sheet from one drawer and wax paper from another. "Possibly better than Cheryl."

"Wow," Brandon said. "Cheryl was great."

"I know."

Again Cameron stared at the chili, deep in thought, as though chili beans might hold the secrets of the universe. You just never knew, Adam thought.

Finally, Cameron looked up and said, "So let me get this straight. You think Mom got Trish a job as a floater, then arranged for Cheryl to quit, then made sure Marjorie put Trish in her place in hopes that you might fall…?"

"When you say it out loud, it sounds pretty farfetched," Brandon admitted as he took a seat at the kitchen table.

Adam bit back an expletive as he formed the first hamburger patty. He watched Cameron stir the chili some more as his brother tried to work out this conundrum.

Cameron added a bit more salt while he muttered, "It doesn't make sense."

"Well, it's Mom," Brandon said, slouching in his chair as he took a long sip of beer.

"I know," Cameron said. "I'm trying to work out all the angles, but I'm coming up with nothing. There's no way she could've pulled this off. It's impossible."

"You sure?" Adam said, his eyes narrowing. Cameron always weighed the odds, studied all the angles. If he said it was impossible…

"I'm absolutely sure." Cameron nodded with conviction. "I mean, Mom's good, but that's really out there."

"Yeah, I know, but…" Adam pounded another lump of hamburger meat into submission and put it on the cookie sheet. "I can't help feeling it's all a little too coincidental."

"You're right," Cameron said as he added more salt and chili powder to the pot. "But how could she have arranged everything? The scenario borders on labyrinthine."

Brandon's eyebrows shot up. "Labyrinthine. Nice."

"Thanks," Cameron said with a nod. "Bottom line, it's impossible."

When the kitchen door opened and Sally popped inside, Adam couldn't help but grin. With her platinum-blond hair pulled back in a ponytail, their mother looked like a teenager in pink shorts, a white tank top and purple flip-flops. "I'm going to set the table, and the girls need more sangria."

"I'll bring another pitcher out in a minute, Mom," Brandon said.

"Thanks, sweetie." Sally began pulling knives and forks out of the drawer, then glanced around at each of the men. "What are you boys cooking up in here?"

Brandon gave her a look of complete innocence. "Chili, Mom."

Sally eyed him suspiciously, then looked at Adam. "Is that all?"

"I was just bringing them up to speed on Fantasy Mountain," Adam said. "We'll be out in a minute."

"I hope so." She grabbed napkins from another drawer and crossed to the backdoor. "It's a beautiful day outside and I don't want you spending it inside talking shop."

"Yes, Mom," all three men said in unison.

As soon as the door shut, Cameron said, "Where were we?"

"Mom's diabolical plot to take over the world as we know it," Brandon said, and pointed his beer bottle at Cameron. "You were saying it's impossible, but Adam still thinks it's a little too coincidental."

"Maybe I'm just being paranoid," Adam said.

"You can blame that on Brandon," Cameron said, grinning.

"Hey," Brandon said, straightening up. "I'm not paranoid, I'm just vigilant."

Cameron's smile faded as he leaned against the stove and crossed his arms. "I want to be clear. When I said it was impossible, I meant that there's no way Mom or Marjorie could've convinced Cheryl to quit. But we all know how determined Mom can be, so it's entirely possible that she had Marjorie scoping out the scene at DDI for possible replacements that might come up at any time, in any of our offices. They could've planted Trish in the floater pool with the intention of using her on any of us."

"And they got lucky with Cheryl," Adam finished.

"Exactly," Cameron said.

"I told you Mom was recruiting her friends to help her," Brandon reminded them. "This is sounding more and more plausible by the minute."

"Dammit." Adam looked at his brothers, each in turn, then said, "Somehow, some way, Mom's behind this. And if she is, then Trish is a willing participant. Which means, my brothers, she's fair game."

Brandon laughed. "You're gonna turn the tables on her."

"That's my plan," Adam said. "I figure if she's looking to seduce me, I'm going to head her off at the pass. I'll seduce *her*. Then, I'll let her know I'm in on her scheme with Mom just before I cut her loose."

"It's good," Cameron said with an approving nod. "I like it."

"It'll work," Brandon agreed with a look at Adam. "As long as you don't slip up."

Adam pierced him with a look. "Please."

"Hey, it's not just you on the chopping block here, bro. If Mom succeeds with you, the two of us are next. You're fighting this battle not just for the Dukes, but for all mankind."

"Amen," Cameron told him.

Brandon stared out the window at their mother and her friends laughing and talking. "They're probably toasting their victory as we speak."

Cameron snorted. "A bit premature to be celebrating, don't you think?"

"Trust me," Adam said through gritted teeth. "They're doomed for disappointment."

Five

"We're cleared for takeoff, Mr. Duke."

"Thanks, Pamela."

As the older flight attendant disappeared behind the partition that separated the passenger compartment from the galley, Adam glanced at Trish sitting next to him. Her face was pale but still lovely. She wore a severe navy business suit with a plain white blouse, yet still managed to appear feminine and sexy. His fingers itched to peel that suit off her as soon as humanly possible. "All buckled up, Trish?"

"Um…" She rechecked the buckle she'd checked six or eight times already. "Yes."

"Good." He glanced at his watch. "We should be there in an hour or so. We can use the time now to discuss the opening-night situation. Did you bring your notes?"

"Yes." She licked her lips as the jet engines began

to roar and the powerful Gulfstream G650 moved into position on the runway. "But if you don't mind, I need a minute or two."

"Why? What's wrong?"

"Nothing," she said, closing her eyes. "I just need a minute."

She gripped the armrests tightly as the jet picked up speed.

"I thought you weren't afraid of flying," he said.

Her jaw clenched. "Not afraid, just alert."

"If you were any more alert, you'd be spinning."

"My seat belt's on," she pointed out. "I won't spin very far."

He leaned in and whispered. "I hope not. I need you right here next to me."

Her eyes sprang open and she glared at him. "Are you trying to distract me?"

"Maybe. Is it working?"

She closed her eyes and settled back. "No."

"I could try harder," he said softly.

"Please don't," she murmured, biting her lower lip. "I'm trying to concentrate."

"On what? Keeping the plane up?"

"Yes," she admitted. "Do you mind?"

"Not at all," he said as he leaned his head back against the headrest. "In fact, I appreciate it."

"You're welcome," Trish said. Her eyes remained closed but a ghost of a smile formed on her lips.

Without thinking, Adam touched her hand to gauge how tense she really was. She immediately grabbed hold of his hand and held on for dear life.

He watched her face as the luxurious private jet soared to cruising altitude. Her demeanor remained serene but her grip on his hand grew more taut until he thought she might cut off the circulation to his fingers.

Then she licked her lips again and he felt his throat grow dry as his stomach tightened in a knot of arousal. He wondered if she would bring this same level of focus to their lovemaking. When he slipped inside her, would she grip him so tightly, he wouldn't know where he left off and she began? Would she call out his name as she reached her peak? Would her eyes flutter closed or would she watch him watching her as they both flew over the edge? He would have his answer soon, of that he had no doubt.

A few minutes later, Adam saw Pamela, the flight attendant, leave her seat. He took it as an indication that the plane had leveled off enough that they were free to move around.

"You can open your eyes now," he said. "Mission accomplished."

She blinked her eyes open and glanced around, then abruptly released his hand. When she realized he was staring at her, she sighed. "I suppose you think I'm nuts."

He smiled indulgently as he unlatched his seat belt. "Not at all."

"Right," she said acerbically, then muttered, "I'm not sure why you needed me to come along anyway."

She might not have seen the point of her presence here today, but Adam did. The point was seduction. He intended to keep her very close to him from now on. He was on a mission of his own and there was no doubt whether he would accomplish it or not. She would be his. His for as long as he desired her. Eventually he would let her know he'd guessed her true intentions and he'd send his sexy gold digger packing.

For now, he sat back in the streamlined chair and assumed a relaxed pose.

"I'll need you to take notes as we survey the problem areas of the parking structure. We'll have to turn those notes into a joint agreement with the lawyers. But I also want your point of view on things in general. You haven't been to the resort so I'd like to hear your first impressions of everything you see."

She thought about that for a moment, then nodded. "I'll do my best."

"I expect nothing less."

She smiled hesitantly. "Thank you."

Pamela arrived with a basket of muffins and croissants with butter and jam, then poured coffee and juice.

He watched Trish choose a flaky croissant, then slather it in butter and jam.

"I told you to order whatever you wanted," he said. "They must have some low-fat frittata thing with gloppy yogurt, or maybe some flavor-free granola? We could ask."

She had the good grace to laugh. "No, I told them I'd have whatever you were having."

"I'm in shock," he admitted, then stared at the rich chocolate croissant on his plate. "This stuff probably isn't the healthiest choice, but it's the easiest, and they taste great."

"We all have to indulge once in a while," she said, then took a bite of the croissant and almost moaned in delight. "Oh, it's so good."

He couldn't look away. She happily ate the entire pastry, savoring each little morsel on her plate. When he caught her licking a drop of jam off her finger, it took every last ounce of willpower he had to maintain self-control and not start licking her fingers himself.

Trish, meanwhile, seemed completely unaware of his precarious state. How was that possible? How could someone who'd agreed to play a part in his mother's matchmaking game be so oblivious to the effect she was having on him?

The only explanation was that she knew exactly what she was doing. It was all an act. Licking jam off her fingers, gripping his hand earlier—it was all part of the game. And if she wanted to play games, he was all for it. But he was the one who would decide precisely what game they'd play.

And the name of this game was hardball.

After twenty minutes of breakfast and business talk, the dishes were cleared and Trish excused herself. She made her way to the airplane's compact bathroom, where she washed her hands, then stared at herself in the mirror.

"What is wrong with you?" she whispered viciously. "Have you gone insane?" She splashed some water in her face to clear her brain before freshening her lipstick. She still couldn't believe she'd grabbed hold of Adam's hand earlier. Yes, she was a nervous flyer, but that was no excuse. He was her boss, for goodness' sake, as well as her sworn enemy.

But it had felt so comfortable and seemed so right to hold on to him. And he didn't appear to have minded at all. In fact, he'd been the one to touch her first, hadn't he? So it wasn't really her fault, was it?

"I don't care who started it," she berated herself, "There will be no more holding hands with the boss."

She needed to maintain some sense of dignity, after all. She still had to get through the day with him, not to mention the trip back home. What would she do for an encore on that flight? Kiss him?

"Oh, don't even go there."

But it was too late. She'd been thinking about it for days, wondering what it would be like to kiss him. How it would feel to be held and touched and made love to by him. Her thighs tingled at the image she'd conjured up and the desire threatened to overwhelm her.

She was in big trouble.

She exhaled heavily, knowing she had to shake those thoughts away. If she fell for Adam Duke, she wouldn't be able to live with the consequences. She wouldn't be able to face Mrs. Collins or Sam Sutter, the bike store owner, or the Mauberts or any of the others, having broken her vow to avenge their pain. She needed to remember their faces, remember her goal, her mission.

Shoring up her nerves, she fluffed her hair and straightened her suit jacket, then made her way back to her seat.

Adam had opened his briefcase while she was gone and was looking over some sort of legal document.

As she sat down, he looked up and shook his head. "I'm reading the specs and they're all correct. The ADA parameters are all spelled out. So why didn't the construction company get it right?"

"Will you consider a lawsuit?" she asked.

He laughed without humor. "We can't exactly sue a company that we own."

She blinked. "You own Parameter Construction?"

"Yeah." He didn't look happy. "Bought 'em last year, along with a few other small companies. We're still working out the kinks."

"Oh. Well, that's a problem, but maybe it won't be as bad as you think."

He shrugged. "We'll know soon enough. No matter what needs to be done, I refuse to delay the opening. The resort is booked to capacity for the entire season. I won't put that in jeopardy."

"Absolutely not," she said indignantly. "They'll just have to make it happen."

"Exactly," he said, then leaned a little closer to add, "I admire your passion."

It was a simple compliment, so why was she suddenly tongue-tied? Did he mean it as a double entendre or was it just her wild imagination again? When he said *passion,* did he mean *passion?* Or did he simply appreciate her enthusiasm for the work? Did it matter? And could she be a bigger dolt? She realized that he was staring again and scrambled desperately to collect her wits back from wherever they'd scattered off to.

"Anyone can see it's the right thing to do," she said weakly.

"Not necessarily," he said, tapping the document. "Some people don't have a problem cutting corners."

"Please fasten your seat belts, Mr. Duke, Ms. James," Pamela said. "We're beginning our descent and should be landing shortly."

Trish's nerves began to race in a whole new direction as she fumbled for the seat belt.

"All buckled up?" he asked, shoving the document back into his briefcase.

"I'm getting there," she said, annoyed to hear the tension in her own voice. Finally, she managed to connect the belt securely around her waist.

Without another word, Adam took her hand in his. The movement pulled her up close to his warm, solid shoulder and her fears gave way to heated cravings. She tried to concentrate on breathing, deeply, evenly, but his strong, masculine scent got in the way. It clouded her mind and turned her thoughts to mush. When he began to stroke her hand softly with his thumb in an apparent effort to calm her, Trish almost melted into a puddle right then and there.

The plane cleared the mountain, then leveled off as it descended toward the Fantasy Mountain airstrip. It could hardly be called an airport, although that was the Dukes' eventual plan for it.

Adam glanced over at Trish and noticed that she'd turned a delicate shade of green. It must've been that sharp bank over the last mountain range that did her in. Was she going to be ill? She had a death grip on his hand and was rubbing her stomach with her free hand. She seemed to be trying to swallow over and over, probably to keep her ears from popping.

A moment ago, a strange protective instinct had made him take hold of her hand in an attempt to reassure her that everything would be okay. Watching her now, he had an irresistible urge to pull her onto his lap, cradle her in his arms and soothe away her fears. But he resisted and the moment passed.

It wasn't his job to comfort her. Yes, it bothered him that she seemed to be suffering, but he had to keep in mind just why she was there in the first place.

Damn, she was the most unlikely gold digger he'd ever met. She should've been more sophisticated, more of a game player. She should've been the sort of woman who was used to flying off to exotic places and carrying on casual, flirtatious conversations with men. But she hardly seemed the type.

He wondered what Sally and Marjorie had promised her in exchange for her part in this charade. Besides Adam Duke, that is. Had they offered her money? A new car? A permanent job with the company?

But Adam knew his mother and the more he thought about it, the more certain he was that his mother would never try to buy off a woman with material goods. No, Mom would figure that marriage to her son would be a good enough lure for any woman.

And Trish had agreed. He supposed he should be flattered, but he wasn't.

Whatever devil's bargain she'd agreed to, she would ultimately fail. In the meantime, though, Adam was more than willing to play along. He would be lying if he said he only wanted to seduce her because of her part in Sally's matchmaking game. No, Adam just plain wanted her. Wanted his hands on her lush curves. Wanted his mouth on her lips, her skin. He wanted to feel her all over, inside and out. It had been this way ever since the first day she walked into his office. And he would have her, all of her. Soon.

And that's where the game would end.

Norman Thompson, the ADA lawyer, had a tendency to drone on and on.

"I've already told you that we'll make the changes, Norm," Bob Paxton said calmly. "Just give us your notes and cut the editorials."

"Did you get that last measurement, Trish?" Adam said, crossing the narrow walkway to stand beside her.

"Yes, I've got it," she murmured, grateful she'd brought a new legal pad with her on the trip. She'd filled almost every page. She was also grateful she'd borrowed

Deb's warm down jacket and thin, thermal gloves or she would've turned into a block of ice by now. Despite the sunny day, it was cold up here in the mountains and they'd been outside for almost five hours.

"Do you have anything more for us?" Adam asked the lawyer.

Thompson snorted in disgust. "Isn't that enough?"

"Yes, it is," Adam said easily. "Thank you for your input. We'll send you a complete list of the changes we make, along with photographs of the completed work. I assume you'll want to conduct a final survey of the grounds after the work is completed."

"Absolutely," he said.

"Good." He glanced from Bob to Trish to the lawyer. "We're finished here."

"I suppose," Thompson said, dropping his own notepad into his thin briefcase. "I'll expect your report within the month."

"You'll get it next week," Adam said briskly, holding out his hand. "Have a good day."

"Well." He shook Adam's hand. "You do the same."

They watched Thompson walk back to his car, then Bob turned to Adam. "Next week might be cutting it close, but we'll aim for it."

"I want it done," Adam said. "If you have any problems with the crew, I want to hear about it immediately."

"There won't be any problems," Bob said determinedly as he put his small, digital camera back in his pocket. "I'll e-mail you the photos as soon as I'm back in my office. And I'll find out exactly who was responsible for all the mistakes."

"I know you will," Adam said, shaking hands with the contractor. "Thanks, Bob."

"It was great to meet you, Bob," Trish said.

"Nice meeting you, too, Trish," Bob said, shaking her hand. Then she and Adam watched him head back to the construction trailer parked on the periphery of the resort property.

"Let's get up to the lodge," Adam said, placing his hand on the small of her back and leading her away from the parking structure. "It's freezing out here."

"I'm glad I'm not the only one who noticed," Trish said, but now she wasn't sure if her shivers were from the weather or from his touch.

As he guided her along the bark-covered shortcut to the lodge, Adam pointed out the beginnings of several trails to be used for cross-country skiing and snowshoeing once the snow began to fall. The downhill skiing trail was just a short hike away.

"It's so beautiful," Trish said, stopping to look in every direction.

"I think so," Adam said gruffly, looking right at her.

Trish felt herself blushing and would've looked away, but how could she? It was as if he were a magnet and she were metal. His eyes were so blue and knowing, so aware of everything. Did he know what she was thinking? What she wanted?

Trish blinked. What was wrong with her? She still couldn't believe she was here in this place with him. When she'd first seen that letter from the ADA lawyer, she wished she'd been the one to alert the man about the problems at the resort. It would've been sweet revenge indeed against Adam Duke. But after hearing Adam talk about the handicapped kids he'd known at the orphanage, she was glad she'd had nothing to do with it. It almost broke her heart to know Adam had spent part of his childhood so lonely and alone.

She was still determined to seek justice and closure. She owed that much to Grandma Anna and the others. But she wouldn't do it on the painful memories of a lonely child living in an orphanage.

There was no sign of that childhood pain now as she stared at Adam and saw the stark hunger in his eyes. Then the starkness disappeared as Adam glanced around the trail.

"Serenity Lake is just beyond the main building," he said, casually pointing over her shoulder as if they hadn't just shared a special, lust-filled moment. "We'll be able to see it from the lodge. In summer and fall, there's boating, kayaking, canoeing, fishing, hiking, bird watching, mountain biking. We also offer yoga, croquet, tennis, golf and horseback riding."

"Wow."

He grimaced. "I sound like a travel agent, don't I?"

She laughed. "Yes, you do. But I'm sold. This place is fantastic."

Trish stared up at the magnificent Arts and Crafts-style resort that rose six stories up the side of the mountain. Fantasy was a perfect name for it. The stone and timber façade, dark wood gables and carved willow balconies offset the forest-green pitched roof, covered walkways and tall stone chimneys. The overall effect was stunning, rustic yet aristocratic.

"It's amazing," she said.

"Wait'll you see the inside," Adam said, grabbing her hand to take her up the wide plank stairs and through the impressive double-door entrance.

"It's…" Trish slowly spun around to take in the massive main lodge. The huge fireplace at one end of the room was tall enough that Trish could walk inside it. She wouldn't, of course, since there was a roaring fire warming the space. But it was certainly big.

Throughout the room, golden brown leather chairs and sofas were grouped around hand-built twig tables. Thick carpets covered the hardwood floors and wide wood beams stretched across the immense cathedral ceiling. The walls were exposed timbers, bleached, then varnished to a rich, warm hue.

"It's dazzling," she said finally.

He chuckled. "Why don't you have a seat by the fire? I'll check where they put our bags and get the keys to our rooms for the night, then we'll take a tour, meet the chef and have dinner."

She stopped in her tracks. "Our rooms? Dinner? Aren't we flying back?"

"It's after four o'clock and we still have work to do here," he explained. "We'll spend the night and go back tomorrow morning. That way you can meet with the chef and we can talk about the opening."

"But that's crazy," Trish said before she could stop herself. "I can't spend the night here with you."

He studied her for a moment. "Is it spending the night away from home that worries you or the fact that you're here with me?"

"Neither," she said hastily. "I'm not worried. I'm just…hmm."

He moved closer and seemed to grow taller, stronger, before her eyes. "We're here to work, not play."

"I know," she whispered.

He was close enough that she could smell his scent, a heady combination of forest, citrus and Oh, dear lord, leather. If she moved another inch, their mouths would meet. It was tempting.

"Are you afraid of me?" he asked quietly.

She tried to laugh, but her throat was too dry. "Don't be silly."

"Because I assure you, Trish. You're in no danger from me."

"Of course not." She smiled weakly.

He stared at her face for another moment, looking for signs of what? Fear? She gave him her best blank look. He nodded once and went off to get the keys. Sinking into a plush leather chair near the warm fire, Trish swallowed uneasily. In no danger from him? Was he serious? Or simply blind? Oh, if he only knew how much danger she was in. She just hoped he would never find out.

Six

After a tour of the lodge and the behind-the-scenes facilities, Adam introduced Trish to Jean Pierre, the head chef. Together with the hotel and restaurant managers, they all sat down to discuss opening-night strategies. After an hour, Adam ended the meeting and took Trish off to enjoy dinner in the resort's most elegant restaurant.

Adam had already explained to Trish that although the resort wasn't yet open to the public, the entire staff was up and running at full power these last few weeks until the official opening. The kitchen prepared meals throughout the day and the waitstaff served them to other employees with the same professionalism they would show to a paying guest. The same procedure was followed by the other departments throughout the hotel, and everything was observed and graded by the management team.

When it came to running their resorts, the Dukes preferred to leave nothing to chance.

And when it came to seducing beautiful women, Adam Duke left nothing to chance, either.

It had occurred to him as he was picking up their room keys, that his strategy with Trish could use some fine-tuning. So far, she was playing the model employee, pretending confusion and uncertainty when he'd informed her they'd be spending the night in this remote, beautiful place. He'd ostensibly played right into her hands, practically delivering himself on a silver platter for her enjoyment. So why hadn't she taken the bait?

Why was she continuing to act so coy?

You'd never know she had her sights set on him, he thought with some disgust. She was obviously playing hard to get, but the goody-goody act was no longer working for him. He would have to find a way to break through her charade. He wanted to look into her eyes and see her hunger, her craving, her need for him.

That's when he would make his move.

Adam had been in the corporate world a long time and his business instincts were well-honed. He knew how to stoke the fires of desire—in both business and pleasure. He was aware that the surest way to drive up both price and demand was to make it clear that the item was unavailable.

It worked in property development, in sales and acquisitions—and it would work with Trish. With that in mind, Adam decided that he would be the one to play hard to get. He would wine and dine and flatter and cajole and work her into such a state of frenzied need that she would be the one to proposition him. And then he would decide whether to say yes or no.

And because he was such a nice guy, he would probably say yes. Make that *hell,* yes.

Accompanying Trish into the dining room, Adam stood close enough to hear her breath catch as he touched her shoulder. He felt her heartbeat flutter as his fingers glided over the pulse point of her wrist. He wondered what she was thinking. Was she as attracted to him as he was to her? Oh sure, she wanted him as a husband, but did she want him as a lover? If so, she was playing it awfully damn cool.

He looked forward to turning up the heat.

They were led to a beautifully set table in front of the wide, plate-glass window overlooking the shimmering lake. As Adam pulled out her chair, he deliberately touched the small of her back, then let his hand glide up to her neck as she sat down. He was pleased to feel her back arch in response, as though she wanted more.

He would not disappoint her.

As Trish gazed at the view, dusk turned to dark and the world outside the window turned magical. She gasped as strategically designed outdoor lighting twinkled to life, accenting the beauty of the nearby forest and surrounding mountains. All of it was reflected in the serene surface of the lake.

"It's so perfect," she said, gazing across the table at him.

"I'm glad you like it," he said, admiring the way her brown hair tumbled loosely around her shoulders and her green eyes sparkled in the candlelight.

"How could anyone not love it?" She smiled dreamily as she placed her napkin in her lap. "If I were you, I'd never want to leave."

Adam was glad he'd arranged in advance to have the stylish restaurant all to themselves. It should've felt odd or eerie to be the only diners, but it didn't. The room was beautiful and well-lit. Willow screens and feathery trees in large pots were used to create intimate dining spaces. The staff was attentive, yet discreet.

Again leaving nothing to chance, Adam had contacted Jean Pierre over the weekend and requested that the chef prepare an extensive tasting menu consisting of those items he was considering serving at the opening-night gala.

For the next two hours, Adam and Trish tasted tiny skewers of tender grilled baby vegetables and savory meats along with a wonderful assortment of delicate canapés. Tiny pancake pillows topped with smoked salmon, crème fraiche and dill, bite-sized pieces of rare roast beef in a pastry crust accompanied by dipping sauces of creamy, homemade horseradish and a savory chutney. There were decadent sauces, fluffy patés and fragile mini-soufflés.

To accompany the hors d'oeuvres, there were six different champagnes to choose from and a number of vintages of cabernet sauvignon to sip and enjoy.

The conversation was enjoyable, as well. Adam found Trish's opinions stimulating and thoughtful, so they had a spirited discussion on a number of issues. They discovered a mutual appreciation of both vintage jazz and the Sunday comics. She had a sense of humor and she was smart and most important, loyal.

When the conversation finally wound around to the issues plaguing the resort, Trish wondered aloud just how the construction snafu might have occurred. She offered to assist Bob with his investigation of the subsidiary that had cut corners.

"When the truth emerges," she said, shaking her finger at him, "heads will roll."

"I'm glad you're on my side," he said, chuckling.

"Oops," she murmured, realizing what she'd said. "I think I've had too much champagne."

"But you're having fun, aren't you?"

"Yes." She smiled. "Everything is just beautiful. Thank you for including me in your evening."

"I had no intention of dining without you." He sipped his wine. "But now I have to ask, why were you so concerned about staying overnight up here? Do you have a boyfriend waiting at home?"

"Good heavens, no."

He was relieved to hear her say so. "A hot date maybe?"

She frowned. "No, of course not."

"Why 'of course not'? Don't you date? You're a beautiful woman."

Despite the soft candlelight, Adam could see Trish's cheeks turn pink.

"You shouldn't say things like that," she said.

"Even if it's true?" Adam teased. His grin faded as he sipped his wine. "Were you nervous about being alone with me?"

She glanced around the room as if she might be looking for the waitstaff. "We're not alone."

He leaned in. "Yes, we are."

Biting her lower lip, she looked around again, then straightened up and gazed directly at him. "No, of course I'm not nervous about being alone with you. You're my boss. I know I'm perfectly safe with you."

He studied her. "I wish I could say the same."

"What do you mean?"

"I'm not sure how safe I am around you."

She swallowed. "Don't be silly."

"You're dangerous to my peace of mind."

Her brow furrowed. "But I'm…I'm harmless."

"Hardly," he said with a grin, then let her off the hook by changing the subject. "Did you grow up around Dunsmuir Bay?"

She hesitated, then said, "Yes."

He chuckled. "You don't sound sure about it."

She raised her chin. "I grew up down by the pier, with my grandmother."

"Oh, yeah?" Adam said, relaxing back in his chair. "I like that area."

"Yes, I loved living there."

"You moved?"

"Yes." She looked away, unwilling to say more.

It sounded to Adam as if there might be more to the story but he didn't push. Instead, he held his glass up, determined to lighten the mood. "Let's have a toast. To Fantasy."

Trish managed a smile as she tapped her glass to his. "To Fantasy." She took a sip, then put the glass down and groaned. "Everything has been delicious, but I can't put one more thing in my mouth."

A vivid image of what else she might do with her mouth almost brought Adam out of his seat. It was absurd. What was it about this woman that made his libido behave as if he hadn't gotten laid in five years? Perhaps it was because he knew they'd come together soon. Very soon, he'd be able to bury himself in her warm depths. It wouldn't be soon enough to suit him or his raging erection, however.

Had he honestly thought he could wait for her to make the first move? Impossible.

He was about to suggest that it was time to go, when Jean Pierre emerged from the kitchen with several small platters and began to explain all the desserts he'd chosen for them. Adam's ardor was effectively extinguished, probably a good thing.

Trish's eyes grew wider with each little morsel the chef pointed to. After he left them alone, she stared at Adam in dismay.

"This is crazy," she whispered. "Seriously, I can't eat another bite."

"I'm not sure I can, either, but we don't want to hurt Jean Pierre's feelings." Adam speared a succulent miniature fruit tart with his dessert fork and held it out for her to taste. "Just one more bite?"

She moaned and rubbed her stomach. "I can't do it."

"But how will we know if it's suitable for the gala?"

"Why don't you taste it?" she asked.

"Because I'm the boss and I say it's your job to taste the desserts."

Trish laughed. "I'm not sure I've ever seen that rule in the employee handbook."

Adam chuckled. "Okay, then do it for Jean Pierre."

"Oh, all right." She took a deep breath. "This is for Jean Pierre."

"Good girl," Adam said, moving the fork closer. "One little taste."

She took the bite and licked her lips. "Mmm, it's really delicious."

Beguiled, Adam scooped a small spoonful of creamy chocolate mousse and held it out for her to sample. "One more bite, babe. Open wide."

"Okay," she said, smiling. "but only because it's chocolate."

"That's my girl," he murmured.

Time stood still as he watched her close her eyes, open her mouth and take the bite. Then she sighed.

"Oh." She licked her lips and moaned. "Oh, my God. Oh, it's fabulous." She swallowed, then licked her lips again.

In an instant, Adam's body was tight and aching. So much for playing hard to get. He wanted her with a need that burned right through him. In his current condition, he'd never make it out of the restaurant alive. Fine with him. He'd send the staff home, then make love to Trish right here.

So much for his grand scheme of withholding sex until she begged for it. He was the one who would beg her if he had to. Without even trying, she was the sexiest woman he'd ever met.

She was saying something, but he couldn't hear her. All the blood that might've helped his brain function had recognized a more urgent need and rushed to his body's lower half.

Adam tossed his napkin on the table and stood. "Let's go," he said, almost growling the command.

"Don't we have to pay the bill first?"

"I own the place, sweetheart." He came around to pull her chair out. "There is no bill."

"I guess I really am tired if I forgot that." She smiled up at him.

But on the way out, she insisted on stopping to thank everyone who'd waited on them, then poked her head into the kitchen and called out her gratitude to Jean Pierre, who came running over to kiss her on both cheeks and thank her profusely.

She had a way of making everyone feel special, including Adam, he thought as he led her out of the restaurant. He was beginning to wonder just exactly who was seducing whom.

Riding up in the elevator, Trish could barely breathe. Her heart raced and she shivered with pleasure, he was standing so close. She should've backed away and cut herself off from his touch, but she couldn't bear to. Not yet. Once they were back in Dunsmuir Bay and reality set in, she would deal with these forbidden emotions. But right now she simply wanted to concentrate on his masculine scent, feel the soft pressure of his arm against hers, appreciate his tall, confident stance and wonder how it would feel to be wrapped up in his arms.

She shivered again.

"You're cold," he said, shrugging off his jacket and slinging it over her shoulders. Then he put his arm around her and pulled her closer. "The mountain air can sneak up on you."

"Thank you," she murmured, wondering if he'd read her mind. If so, couldn't he see that it wasn't the cold making her shiver? Good grief, she was burning up—couldn't he feel it? But it felt so good to be pressed against his hard body, she never wanted him to stop holding her.

Even though she knew it didn't mean anything. Could *never* mean anything. He was just being polite, after all.

Trish made an effort to keep her thoughts casual as she glanced around the elevator. Even in this small space, the hotel's rustic style prevailed, with a charming bench to sit on and kitschy antler sconces on the walls.

There had been a few times during dinner when she thought Adam might be attracted to her, thought he might even be tempted to kiss her good-night. But he was all business now, holding himself rigid even though he had his arm around her. It was just as well. She had no business thinking they could ever be more to each other than boss and assistant. And, lest she forget, she still had her mission to accomplish, even though at the moment, she could barely remember what that mission was.

It must've been the champagne, or maybe the chocolate mousse. She wasn't thinking clearly at all.

They left the elevator at the top floor and Adam stopped at a door halfway down the hall. Using a card key, he opened the door and held it for her to walk inside.

"Oh," she said on a quick intake of breath as she looked around the large king-size hotel room, then walked directly to the stone fireplace. A fire had been set recently and was going strong, radiating warmth throughout the room.

There were throw pillows piled on the wide stone hearth for cozying up close by the fire, and the mantel held a sweet display of old-fashioned portraits in small Victorian frames. Hanging on the walls on either side of the mantel were vintage tinted photographs of mountain and lake scenes.

"So pretty," she murmured, then turned away from the fireplace and noticed the carved wood king-size bed for the first time.

"Wow." It was a masterpiece, covered in richly brocaded silk with a colorful cluster of pillows. Whole logs made up the frame and headboard, and tall, braided willow branches acted as bedposts. The willows were adorned by gauzy drapes that looped from one branch to the next, giving the room a light, ethereal feel.

The room smelled of pinecones and forest rain. She breathed it all in.

"I'm in awe," she said, spinning around to see more. "I love it."

"I'm glad." He leaned against the sliding-glass door leading to the balcony. His arms were folded across his chest and he looked relaxed and confident and too sexy for her own good, Trish thought.

He unlocked the glass door and stepped outside. "I know it's cold, but you should come out and see the view."

She joined him, grateful for the chilly air. Maybe it would cool off the heat washing through her. Adam stood at the rail, staring out at the lake and the mountain rising on the opposite side—dark, vast and mysterious. The moon had risen and was reflected in the water's surface.

"It takes my breath away," she said. "I wish we could stay for a week."

"Do you?"

"Who wouldn't?" she demurred. "It's lovely."

"So are you."

She looked away. "No, I'm not."

"You take my breath away," he said slowly, his dark eyes shining with intent.

She looked up at him, in time to see him lower his head to hers. In time to tell herself to stop this.

"Adam, I'm not sure…" Trish's thoughts scattered as he covered her mouth with his. His lips were soft yet demanding and the thrill was instant, the warmth so all-consuming, she wondered if she might go up in flames.

"You're not sure what?" Adam murmured against her skin as his mouth traveled along her jawline.

Trish barely heard him through the cloud of sensation fogging her mind. "What?"

His deep chuckle reverberated as his hand cupped the nape of her neck. "I'm going to kiss you again."

She was aware of her heart pounding rhythmically in her chest as she pressed her hand against him. "You shouldn't."

He met her gaze. "You don't want me to kiss you?"

"Whether I want you to or not isn't the point," she whispered.

"Then it's settled," he said, and returned to ravage her mouth.

The vague thought that nothing was settled flitted away. A soft moan escaped her and her knees nearly crumpled as his tongue urged her to open for him. She obliged him, wanting to taste him, wanting to feel his touch everywhere on her body. He was all heat and hardness as he pressed against her. The world around her dissolved and all that mattered was his mouth on hers, his hands gripping her backside as he aroused and devoured her.

"Oh, Adam, I…"

"I want to make love with you, Trish," he said, his dark blue eyes gleaming.

She gulped and felt the last of her resolve drain away. "I—I want that, too, Adam."

"I'm glad," he said. "It's cold. Let's go inside."

He took her hand and led her back inside and slid the door closed. Still holding her hand, he walked to the bed, where he stopped, kissed her again with slow deliberation, then released her only to pick up his jacket and tuck it under his arm.

"What are you doing?" she asked.

"I'm saying good night."

She couldn't have heard him right. "You're what?"

"Saying good night," he said, cupping her cheek in the palm of his hand and stroking her skin with his thumb. "And thanking you for a fantastic evening."

He kissed her again and she met him with fervor and a need she'd never experienced before.

"But…but you can't go," she said, still not believing him. How could he get them both so wound up only to walk away? How could he kiss her, tell her he wanted to make love with her and then leave?

"Believe me, I don't want to," he said, resting his forehead on hers and staring into her eyes. "But I also don't want to rush you into something you might regret later."

She almost groaned, knowing she should be grateful for his thoughtfulness. Knowing she should appreciate that he was willing to take it slow. Knowing that she didn't want him to leave.

"But I warn you that the next time we kiss," Adam said, skimming his lips against hers, "it won't stop there."

He pulled back to meet her gaze. "And there *will* be a next time."

She blinked, stunned into silence by his words.

"Sweet dreams, sweetheart," he said, drawing her close. His hands skimmed down her back to her hips as his mouth hovered an inch from hers. She parted her lips in invitation but instead of kissing her, he whispered, "Until next time."

Then he opened the door and walked out, leaving her dazed and aching with need.

Seven

I must be out of my mind, Adam thought as the plane soared above the mountains and headed for home. He'd had her just where he wanted her and hadn't made a move. And though he could stand back and marvel at his own inner strength, he had to question whether he'd made a mistake or not. His body was still clamoring for her despite knowing that she was trying to play him.

Now, as he watched Trish squeeze her eyes shut and clutch his hand, Adam wondered if it was indeed inner strength or just plain *stupidity* that had caused him to walk away from her. Last night's kiss had proven that Trish wanted him as much as he wanted her. Sure, maybe she was a gold digger, but he didn't think she'd been faking the need he'd seen in her eyes. And if the look in her eyes hadn't been enough, she'd actually said so. *Out loud,* he reminded himself, replaying the moment over and over in his head. His memory was perfect, dammit. He could recall with absolute clarity the scent of her. The feel of her. The shine in her eyes as she looked up at him. And he could hear her whispered voice echoing in his mind.

I want that, too, she'd said, when he told her he wanted to make love with her.

I want that, too.

So, was he deaf, as well as stupid? She'd *wanted* him. And what had he done? He'd walked away. As a show of strength. To prove that he was his own man and to show the world that no one but Adam Duke would determine his own future. Certainly not some cute-as-hell gold digger. And definitely not his mother.

But what had he gotten for his troubles? A sleepless night, an aching body and a temper on the edge of snapping. Why the hell did it have to be Trish James who appealed to him on every level?

He'd walked away to prove that he wasn't the kind of man who would roll over and play dead just because Trish James said she *wanted* him.

"So how's that whole 'determine your own future' thing working for you?" Adam muttered under his breath. Then he shook his head, thoroughly disgusted. "It's not working well at all."

Because he hadn't determined anything, he told himself. In making his choice to thwart his mother's matchmaking attempts, he'd been *reacting,* not acting. He hadn't made the choice he'd wanted to make. He'd made the only one he *could* make. So, really, his interfering mother and the gold digger she'd set on his scent were still in charge. And the knowledge of that was enough to kick his determination into high gear. There was no way they would win this game. No way at all.

"Did you say something?" Trish asked, her eyes fluttering open.

"No," he said, irritated that she'd caught his muttering. "Just thinking out loud."

She nodded, then looked down at their hands and carefully pulled hers away. "Sorry. But thanks for the hand-holding. Again."

He refused to acknowledge that he missed the feel of her hand in his. Clearly, he was still wound too tightly.

"Whatever gets us off the ground," he said, smiling though his jaw was tense enough to crack walnuts.

"It seems to work." She smiled shyly, then didn't seem to know what to do next, so she pulled out her notes from yesterday, opened her laptop and began typing.

He watched her slim, graceful hands strike the keys, then glanced up to see her squint as she studied her notes. Absorbed in her work, she began to nibble at her bottom lip in concentration, and Adam had the most maddening urge to pull her into his arms and nibble that lip for her. Dragging her off to join the Mile-High Club probably wouldn't be the most professional way to start the business day, but at this point he really didn't care.

The jet leveled off and Adam forced himself to open his briefcase and get some work done. If he could focus on upcoming concerns, maybe his mind would stop wandering to Trish. He pulled out the documents he needed to study for a meeting later this afternoon and tried to concentrate on them. But it was impossible with Trish sitting so close to him. He glanced over and saw her staring at her computer screen, now filled with her notes from yesterday's survey with the ADA lawyer. She looked fresh and businesslike this morning in a blue-gray suit and a simple white shirt. She hadn't pulled her hair back so it hung loose and thick and wavy around her shoulders and she wore some sultry perfume that wafted into his brain and turned his thoughts to soggy oatmeal.

Who was he trying to fool? There's no way he was going to get any work done. He wanted her more now than he had the night before, which he wouldn't have thought possible. Now that he'd tasted her, he knew it was only a matter of time before he would have all of her.

A matter of time? No. He wanted her now. Wanted his hands on her curvaceous breasts, wanted his mouth on every single inch of her skin. He was rampant at the image of those long, shapely legs wrapped around him. Muttering a harsh expletive under his breath, he subtly adjusted himself in his chair.

He would have her tonight, of that he was certain. There would be no walking away from her this time.

With that settled, Adam ruthlessly squelched his desire for Trish and forced himself to get down to the business of running his company.

"This has got to be the longest day in history," Trish muttered as she sat at her desk later that afternoon. She'd been trying all day to forget about the night before, forget about that stunning kiss and focus on her job.

Earlier, she'd actually considered claiming she was ill and going home. But if she'd gone home, she'd just be staring at her four walls and slowly driving herself insane. But being here at the office, so close to Adam and not being able to do anything about it, was driving her batty.

"And just what would you do about it if you could?"

she asked herself bitterly. "He doesn't want you, remember? You were practically begging him to make love with you and he walked out."

Granted, she didn't have much experience in making love, or with men in general, for that matter. But she was fairly certain that having the man walk out after the woman said she was all fired up and ready to go was not a good sign.

She cringed at the memory of her puckering up and practically begging him to kiss her before he left her room last night. But no. Instead of kissing her, he'd whispered, "Next time," then walked out.

What had he meant? Next time? Next time when? Tonight? Tomorrow? Next *year?* And why did she care? She wasn't here to be romanced. But in spite of her best-laid plans and against her better judgment, she wanted to be.

Needless to say, she hadn't slept well at all last night, despite the beautiful room and that plush bed.

Now she wondered, not for the first time, whether she should just quit her job with Adam Duke and deal with the pain of losing her home and her grandmother in some other way. She had to face the fact that the man she'd been seeking revenge from, the man who had ruined her life and destroyed her grandmother's dream, no longer stirred up the same anger and resentment inside her.

No, that man stirred up something very different inside her now.

"Oh, my goodness," Trish said, as tendrils of lust radiated through the pit of her stomach. She was in very deep trouble if simply thinking about the man could turn her insides to jelly.

Trish forced herself to remember that she was being

paid to work here and that's just what she needed to do. If nothing else, it would keep her from feeling sorry for herself. There was nothing worse than a pity party for one.

Bouncing up from her chair, she gathered a stack of documents that needed to be copied and carried them to the copier. For the next three hours, she buried herself in work, typing documents and letters, making copies, running to the mailroom. Thankfully, the work kept all her troubling thoughts from circling over and over in her mind.

The next time she looked up from her computer, Adam was staring at her from his doorway. "Do you mind staying late tonight? We've got some extra work to take care of."

"No, I don't mind," she said. "I'd planned on it. Shall I order dinner?"

"In a minute," he said. "Can you come into my office first?"

"Of course." It would give her a chance to tell him what she'd been thinking about all day.

He sat on the edge of his desk as she approached.

"I want to thank you for everything," she said tentatively. "Dinner last night was wonderful, the resort is magnificent and, um, I hope you'll accept my apology for what happened, you know, after."

Adam studied her for several long seconds, his face an expressionless mask. "No."

Okay, she hadn't expected that. Couldn't he see how hard it was for her to humiliate herself in front of him? *Again?* As confused as she was by his reaction, she was also a little steamed. For heaven's sake, she was apologizing to him, the least the man could do was be gracious about it.

"No?" Her eyes narrowed in puzzlement. "You won't accept my apology? But…you can't just say no."

"Yes, I can." He pushed away from the desk and approached her. He was so close and his look was so focused on her that for a moment, she thought he might kiss her again, right there in his office. And however crazy it was to think it, it was even crazier to hope he would do it. Which made her wonder just how unhinged she'd become.

But instead of kissing her, he took hold of her hand and led her to the sitting area at the far end of his office.

When they were both seated on the soft burgundy leather couch, Adam squeezed her hand. "Are you apologizing for our kiss last night?"

She couldn't meet his gaze but instead concentrated on an intriguing spot on the wall beyond his left shoulder. "I behaved completely unprofessionally. I can't even believe I did that. You should probably fire me, but maybe we could just move on and forget it ever happened."

"If anyone should apologize, it's me," he told her, dropping her hand and standing up. "I'm your boss. You don't owe me anything."

He pulled her to her feet, took her hands in his and held them tightly. "I should apologize, but I'm not going to."

"You're not?" She blinked at him. This wasn't going the way she'd expected it to.

"No. Because I'm not sorry at all. I really liked kissing you and I'd love to do it again, but I'll understand if you don't want to."

"Oh, but I do," she said in a rush, then felt her cheeks

burn. Very smooth, Trish, she told herself. Burble over him like a high school girl talking to the football star.

"I'll understand," he repeated quickly as his mouth spread into a grin. "I'll be extremely irritable and I'll have to take a cold shower or two, but I'll understand."

She breathed in, then out, slowly. "You'll understand."

"That's right. I won't like it, but you say no and this is done. Here. Now."

She pulled her hands away and tried to gather her thoughts. All she had to do was say no. It was up to her. He wanted her, just as she'd hoped. And she wanted him desperately, despite knowing what kind of man he was. Despite knowing it was a huge mistake. But, first, she had to say something.

"Adam, it's important that you know that I've never done that before. That is, I mean, I hope you don't think I'm…" She exhaled heavily and waved her hand in exasperation. "Oh, you know what I mean."

He laughed softly. "Are you trying to say you don't usually kiss the boss?"

She raised her chin and met his gaze. "Of course I don't."

He gazed at her with that crooked, boyish grin of his and she felt another unwelcome spark burst into flame in her belly. She reminded herself that she was flirting with the enemy, but it didn't help douse the flames. She wanted him. She knew better, knew she should stand up and walk out right then, but she couldn't. She wasn't going anywhere.

"Say no and we're done. But if you don't say it, Trish," he whispered, lifting one hand to skim her hair back from her face, "then there's no stopping once we start."

"I don't want to stop," she confessed, and closed her eyes as his fingertips trailed across her cheek.

He pulled her tight against him and covered her mouth completely in a hot, open-mouthed kiss that overwhelmed and inflamed her.

He held the nape of her neck firmly, keeping her close as their tongues tangled and parried in a wildly sensual paso doble. Trish met his passion with her own ardent desire, ignoring the voice in her head that warned her that if she wanted to survive, *she should walk away from Adam Duke, now.*

But how could she walk away when she was already lost in this sweeping rush of sensation and wanting? Already lost in the softness of his lips that belied the strength and confidence of his lean, hard body. He pressed her against his solid chest, causing her nipples to quiver and harden.

Oh, God, no, she wouldn't walk away.

"Adam, I…" She couldn't complete the thought but it didn't matter as he seemed to anticipate her every want.

"I know," he whispered, and laid her down on the wide couch. He covered her body with his and his mouth claimed hers with renewed urgency. His taste filled her senses, his taut body tempted hers. She could feel him lengthen and harden against her thigh and she wanted all of it, all of him.

She reached up to wrap her arms around his neck at the same time as his hand moved to cup her breast, drawing a soft moan from deep in her throat. He began to unbutton her blouse while his lips nipped and kissed their way along her jaw to her ear, then down her neck.

He pushed himself up and straddled her, staring at

her with a heated intensity that somehow gave her the courage to act more boldly than she felt. He watched intently as she eased her blouse off, then began to unhook her bra.

"I'll do it," he said huskily, and peeled back the white lace cups. His nostrils flared as he stared at her exposed breasts.

"Beautiful," he said, then took both breasts in his hands and used his thumbs to gently flick her nipples to a hard peak.

She caught her breath when he bent down and took her into his mouth, teasing one ultrasensitive nipple first with his teeth, then with his tongue, rolling and licking her firm tip until she groaned aloud.

He continued his tender assault on her other breast as he reached to unzip her pants and ease them down her legs. She took over, shimmying and finally kicking her pants to the floor to allow him full access to every part of her.

His eyes met her gaze and Trish saw a flicker of heat and pure masculine satisfaction in his dark eyes. He slipped his fingers beneath the elastic band of her thong and touched her most intimate spot. When he slid one finger inside her, she gasped.

"So hot and tight," he murmured, then eased out and back in again. He repeated the action over and over, creating friction against her sensitive flesh that aroused and devastated her.

"Adam," she whispered. "Please."

Instead of answering, he stood and made fast work of taking his shirt off, tearing off his shoes and socks before unzipping and removing his trousers.

Trish watched, mesmerized as she savored the sight of his long, powerful legs and well-toned body. She shivered with anticipation and her breath hitched as he pulled off his boxers and revealed his large, stiff erection.

She ached to touch him.

He was watching her now as he reached for his pants and pulled a foil packet from the pocket. He tore it open and slipped on protection, then stretched out on the couch and took her in his arms. He kissed her fiercely, carnally, at the same time as he found her moist core and entered her with one, strong thrust.

Trish's eyes opened wide and she cried out, but almost as quickly as the pain came, it was gone, replaced by a feeling of fullness, an intimate connection she'd never experienced before.

Adam stopped, held perfectly still, locked inside her and stared down into her eyes. "A *virgin?*" His words were strangled as if there were a fist clamped around his throat. "Why didn't you tell me?"

"Can we talk about this later?" she demanded, lifting her hips, drawing him deeper.

He hissed in a breath through gritted teeth.

"Don't stop," she commanded, and latched her ankles over his legs.

He gave her a tight grin. "I have no intention of stopping, but we'll talk about this."

"Later," she moaned. Her hands glided over his shoulders in an attempt to calm him down, urge him on, reassure him it was okay to keep going. *Please* keep going.

His lips found hers again and he kissed her tenderly as he began to move again. Pleasure grew and spread through her and she relaxed beneath him.

"Wrap your legs around me, sweetheart," he murmured. "Move with me."

She did so, matching his rhythm. She could feel his heart pounding against hers and it made her feel alive. She watched his face—beautiful, strong, straining as he gave her pleasure. She tightened her legs around him, then lost sight of everything but the lush heat that was threatening to consume her.

"Open your eyes," he said. "I want to see them turn dark when you come with me."

She was helpless to do otherwise as he plunged and filled her. Heat built within her and need ignited every nerve ending as she climbed higher and higher. She cried out his name as color exploded behind her eyelids and electric pulsations coursed wildly through her body.

Adam stiffened above her and shouted her name. He drove into her one last time, so deeply that she could've sworn she felt him touch her heart. Then he collapsed against her and his full weight pressed her into the couch. He murmured words she couldn't hear, but his warm breath against her skin soothed her.

For the next few minutes, all she could feel were the tremors moving in waves throughout her body and all she could hear was their ragged breathing. She was completely drained and satiated. She felt free, joyfully free and more alive than she'd ever been before.

Eight

Adam carefully shifted and stretched out alongside Trish. He tucked her closer to him and then, leaning on one elbow, stared down at her.

"Why didn't you tell me?"

Despite the fact that they were inches away from each other, she wouldn't meet his gaze. A virgin? Was she really that hungry to get her hands on his bank account that she'd given up something so precious?

Adam wondered what she was thinking. Was she getting ready to bolt? He wouldn't put it past her, but he wasn't about to let her walk out right then. Not until he knew what was going on. He wanted—no, he *needed*—to know what was going through her mind. If she'd felt so compelled to apologize for one measly kiss the night before, she must be drowning in guilt and regret now, after just having had wild, incredible sex on his office couch.

But that didn't mean she was going anywhere. No way. Not yet. His own guilt had ratcheted up a notch or two besides. Would he have taken her if he'd known she was a virgin? No. But that ship had sailed. Besides, he couldn't say why, but he wasn't ready to let her go. Not until he could taste her again. He thought of the private bathroom connected to his office, with a shower big enough for two. He could offer her the use of the shower, then join her there.

The soft curve of her thigh was nestled against his shaft, causing it to stir to attention. He almost groaned aloud. It wasn't bad enough that he'd taken her here, in his office, on the couch. Now he wanted her again.

"I'd better be going," she whispered.

"No," he said immediately, telling himself she was too vulnerable right now for him to allow her to leave—and he refused to dwell on why he cared one way or another. He'd never wanted a woman to stay with him any longer than absolutely necessary. But Trish was different. He wasn't prepared to say how or why she was different. She just was. Gold digger or not, he felt something for her. And besides, he wanted answers to some questions.

"You're not going anywhere until I find out why you didn't tell me you were a virgin."

"Why does it matter?" she asked, still averting her gaze.

"Because I wouldn't have taken you on a damn couch, that's why."

She glared at him. "Well, then, that's why I didn't tell you."

He frowned as he brushed a strand of hair back from her face. "But I could've gone slowly and not hurt you so much."

"You didn't hurt me," she insisted softly, shaking her head as she said it. Her eyelids fluttered and she finally smiled at him. "Well, not too much anyway. And after a few seconds, it was perfect."

"Not yet," he said with determination. "But it will be."

Trish sat at her desk early the next morning, torn between preening like a satisfied cat and crawling under her desk to hide in shame.

She'd had sex with the enemy.

If it had only happened once, she might've chalked it up to temporary insanity. But it hadn't happened just once. Not even twice. *Three times!* In three different ways. She shivered at the memory of everything he'd done to her. One thing was certain: she'd never look at his conference table the same way again. And she was considering erecting a small shrine in front of that awe-inspiring couch of his.

She knew it was wrong, knew what a mistake she'd made, but it had been amazing, wonderful, thrilling. She'd reveled in Adam's kisses, each caress and every whispered word. He'd made her feel like she'd never felt before.

Well, of course she'd never felt those things before. Up until last night, she'd been a virgin.

She couldn't have told Adam why she was still a virgin at the ripe old age of almost twenty-six, so it was a good thing he never asked. She'd grown up sheltered, surrounded and protected by her grandmother and her neighbors at the Victorian Village. Once she went off to college, she was working too hard to mix in much with the party crowd.

She graduated a year early, then came home and

enrolled in the MBA program at the local university. Grandma Anna was starting to slow down, so Trish tried to help out in the store every day. She took over the purchasing and handled all the shipments. She rotated the displays and dealt with advertising and promotions.

Grandma was always teasing her, telling her to go out and meet people, have fun, fall in love. And Trish always figured there would be plenty time to do just that.

But that was around the same time her grandmother and their neighbors applied for historic landmark designation for the Victorian building. And that's when their world came crashing down, thanks to Adam Duke's company.

That's why she was here. Because Adam Duke had destroyed their lives and now she was out to ruin him. If only she could remember that.

Trish sighed heavily and powered up her computer. It was still early enough that she could do some personal work without feeling too guilty.

"This is for you, Grandma," she murmured, then logged onto the company's Web site and did a search of their mergers and acquisitions over the past two years. She made a list of the companies Duke had acquired, and planned to search the Internet to see if any unsavory dealings had gone on during the transactions. She might even try to set up some interviews of the former employees of those companies to see how badly they were treated by the Dukes.

She sat back in her chair, feeling better now that she'd taken some small action toward avenging her grandmother. After the way she'd spent the previous evening, she wasn't sure she'd ever lose these feelings of guilt, but at least she could tell herself that her mission was still on track. She owed that much to her Village friends.

So why did her thoughts keep drifting back to Adam?

This morning it seemed that all she could remember was Adam's skillful moves, his talented mouth and the scent of his skin. Suddenly her loins tightened and fresh waves of excitement surged through her. She could barely suppress a moan.

"Oh, good grief," she muttered as she stood up. She had to get busy. What if someone caught her day-dreaming at her desk? What if *Adam* caught her? It was still early and he wasn't in yet, but he'd be walking down the hall any minute. She swept up a handful of correspondence and rushed off to the copy room to work.

Standing in front of the copy machine, Trish realized she had some serious decisions to make. Where would she go from here? What would she do? She leaned against the machine, closed her eyes and exhaled wearily. It was time to admit that she was in deep trouble.

After all, it wasn't bad enough that she'd slept with the man she'd once considered her worst enemy, the man she'd held responsible for destroying her happiness and the life of her beloved grandmother. And it wasn't bad enough that the man she'd slept with was her *boss,* the person whose company she'd infiltrated in order to destroy him. And it wasn't even bad enough that she'd made a promise to her grandmother on her deathbed that she would avenge the wrongs done to Grandma Anna and her neighbors, that she would find a way to make Adam Duke experience the same level of pain that she and Grandma Anna had known.

No, what was really, really bad was that she couldn't wait to be in his arms all over again.

But it couldn't happen again.

The copy machine stopped and Trish jolted at the abrupt silence. In that moment it became crystal clear exactly what she would have to do. A switch had been thrown inside her conscience. Even though she hadn't gotten a lot of sleep last night and now felt as though she were walking through a heavy fog, she knew at last the direction she must take. Deathbed promises were not to be treated lightly. She'd betrayed not only her grandmother but all her old neighbors by becoming involved with Adam Duke.

How could she ever face her old friends again?

There was only one thing to do.

She had to tell him she could never have sex with him again. If she didn't put a stop to it now, her goal of righting the wrong she'd set out to do would have to be written off as a total failure. Which meant that it wouldn't be Adam who was destroyed. It would be Trish.

As she walked back to her desk with the stack of copies, she concluded that she would talk to Adam as soon as possible. It shouldn't be difficult. After all, why would he care that she was refusing to sleep with him again? He had a million women waiting in line for the same opportunity.

She wrinkled her nose at the thought. Even if that was true, she didn't like to think about all the women in the world who were chomping at the bit for a chance to have wild jungle sex with Adam Duke. It was downright depressing.

As she sat down at her desk and began to check her e-mails, she shook her head in dismay. All those women.

Just waiting in line. Why in the world would he even give a hoot that plain old Trish James would never make love with him again?

"No, absolutely not." Adam had heard enough. He stormed across the office and halted within a foot of her. "I refuse to accept your resignation. You're still my assistant, Trish. There's work to do. So, go back to your desk and do…something."

"Do something?" she repeated, then had the nerve to smile at him.

"You heard me," he grumbled. "Go." He waved his hands as if to shoo her away. Dammit, he couldn't be this close to her without inhaling her luscious scent. He wanted to strip her naked and nail her against the wall. Probably not a good idea to bring that up, given her present mood.

"Adam, please," she said patiently, as if she were a wise parent and he a recalcitrant child. "I didn't say I was resigning. I said I'd been rethinking my job here at DDI."

"Yeah, I heard you," Adam said, crossing his arms tightly across his chest. "I just don't know what the hell you're talking about. Rethinking. I'll probably be sorry I asked, but what the hell's that supposed to mean?"

"It means that things have become complicated," she said carefully. "It means I don't think we should…" she huffed out a breath and fisted her hands against her thighs in frustration. "Do I really have to spell it out for you?"

He took another small step toward her. "Yeah, Trish. Spell it out for me."

"We can't have sex again," she shouted, then

slapped her hand over her mouth and stared at him in astonishment.

"Okay." He grimaced and rubbed his ear. "I don't think they heard you down on the third floor."

"See what you made me do? I didn't mean to yell." The apology was a bit muffled as she still had her mouth covered.

"That's okay," he said, and reached for the hand covering her mouth to coax it away. "I don't agree with your 'rethinking' plan but I appreciate your honesty."

"You do?"

"Of course I do," he said, keeping a strong grip on her hand. "And I've got to say, I also appreciate your feelings."

"Really?" She gave him a suspicious sideways glance. "Well, thank you."

He nodded. "You're welcome. And I'm really glad you're not quitting."

"I would never leave you in the lurch."

"I'm glad." He stroked her shoulder paternally. "I need you, Trish."

She nodded earnestly. "I know. And I won't let you down."

He continued the stroking, gradually moving his hand up to cradle the back of her neck. "You never have."

"Um." She craned her neck ever so slightly to allow him more access. "Thank you, Adam."

"No problem."

"Okay." She bit her bottom lip, then said, "Well then, I guess I'll just go…do…something."

"Yeah, one thing before you go," he said, then bridged the short distance between them by tugging her close to him.

"Um, what are you doing?" she asked warily as they stared at each other.

"Just testing a theory," he said, and nipped gently at her ear. It was gratifying to hear her moan.

"But—"

"You see," he murmured as he ran slow, nibbling kisses along her jaw. "In the interests of full disclosure, I should tell you that I absolutely do intend to have sex with you again."

"Oh," she said, breathing out a sigh as he licked the pulse point at the base of her neck. "But really, that's not a good idea. And I—I should get back to…um, work."

"Yeah, me, too," he said, eliciting a strangled sob from her as he cupped her breast through her silk blouse. "I won't keep you too long."

She arched her back, then groaned, "How can this be happening again?"

"I'll show you," he said, and covered her mouth with his in a devastating kiss that left no doubt about his intentions. Dammit, he'd missed the taste of her. Now he wanted to savor every inch of her skin, inside and out. In seconds, he was reaching to unzip her pants while she fumbled for his belt.

He'd thought after one night that he would've had his fill of her. He'd figured he'd be calling her bluff this morning, revealing her to be the gold digger that she was. But as soon as Trish had tried to call it quits, he'd known he wasn't ready to end it with her. The fact that she'd tried to end it first was something he'd have to think about.

Was she playing him? Was she deliberately being coy in hopes that he'd be the one to push for a relationship? A relationship that would lead to him standing at the altar watching her walk down the aisle?

While that vision should've been enough to send him running for cover, it didn't matter right now. He still wanted her, still needed her with a bone-deep passion that was relentless. And until the need faded, he wasn't about to let her go.

"Adam, touch me," she whispered.

"Glad to," he said. Picking her up, he walked her backwards, then pressed her against the wall and urged her to wrap her legs around his waist. "On second thought, I'm keeping you here all morning."

Her office telephone rang at five o'clock. Trish ran back to her desk, recognized Adam's cell phone number and grabbed the phone.

"Hey, Trish," he said, his deep voice sending waves of desire through her entire body. How could the sound of his voice make her so weak? Oh, she was such a goner.

"Listen," he continued, "I'd like you to stop by my house and drop off the Spirit file on your way home from work tonight. Will that be a problem?"

"No problem at all." Trish slid back into her chair and mentally smacked herself. Work. He was calling about work. What had she expected? He was her employer, remember? She worked for him. For goodness' sake, she really needed to get a life.

"If you don't have plans," he continued, "I can pay you back by cooking dinner."

Dinner? He wanted to cook her dinner? She knew she should say no. It was inviting trouble to continue seeing him. And dinner at his house? Oh, please, she would never make it home. *Come on, Trish. You can do it. Open your mouth and say, no. Say thanks, but no thanks.*

"I really shouldn't," she hedged, and wanted to kick herself for not being firmer in her refusal.

"Do you have plans already?"

Tell him yes!

"Uh, no," she said, then rolled her eyes. What was wrong with her? Why didn't she just lie? Because he would've seen right through it. She was a really bad liar, just as Deb always told her.

"Then stay for dinner."

"I just don't think it's a good idea."

"I thought you were into health and nutrition."

"I am," she said, frowning. What did that have to do with anything?

"You need to eat dinner," he cajoled. "It's not good to skip meals."

She shook her head. "I'm not skipping—"

"Look, Trish, you're bringing me work files. It's just business. I'd like you to stay for dinner so we can discuss the opening-night festivities."

She sighed. "Yes, okay, fine." *You wimp!*

"Great," he said jovially. "I'll grill some steaks. See you in a while."

She placed the phone down, then her head hit her desk with an audible thunk. What was wrong with her? What part of *we can't have sex again!* did she not understand? Of course, as soon as she'd thrown those words at him this morning, he'd taken up the challenge. And she'd bent to his will like a floppy licorice stick. But oh, God, that frenzied round of wild sex against his office wall? Sweet Georgia Brown, for as long as she worked for DDI, she would always look fondly on that particular wall.

"Excuse me," a soft, female voice said. "Is Adam Duke here?"

With a start, Trish lifted her head. She hadn't realized anyone was here, hadn't heard that woman's footsteps because of the thick carpet that covered the wide hallway.

"Hello." Trish stood, straightened her jacket and brushed her hair back as she surreptitiously studied the woman who was several inches shorter than Trish and definitely more voluptuous. She didn't recognize her and wondered who she might be. A client, maybe? The woman wore a lovely coral halter dress that accentuated her remarkable cleavage, and her perfectly highlighted blond hair was pulled up in a sexy updo. She was beautiful and from the looks of her diamond-encrusted watch, buttery soft taupe purse and matching open-toe high heels, she was wealthy, as well.

"I'm sorry," Trish said. "Mr. Duke is not available."

"Oh, dear," the woman said. "Are you sure?"

"Yes."

She sighed. "I was told he worked late most evenings, so I took a chance, hoping he might be available for cocktails tonight." She opened her purse and handed Trish a business card. "I guess we'll do it another night."

"Are you a friend of Adam's?" Trish asked warily as she gripped the business card. Even the woman's stationary was expensive.

"I'm Brenda," she said smoothly. "He'll know who I am. Are you sure he won't be back tonight?"

"I'm afraid not," Trish said. "He's gone for the day."

Brenda sighed again and glanced at her elegant watch. "Tonight really would've been ideal."

"I'll be glad to give him your card."

"Please do," she said, then flashed a knowing smile. "He'll want to know I came by."

"Of course, he will."

"Okay, then." She turned to leave, then stopped and looked back at Trish. She hesitated, then said, "Please let him know that I'm really looking forward to getting to know him better."

Trish smiled tightly. "I'll be sure to tell him."

"Thank you," Brenda said, then walked away.

"No, no, thank you," Trish murmured as she watched the woman stroll down the hall.

The potatoes were baking in the oven, the wine was opened and breathing, the steaks were marinating. As the doorbell rang, Adam put the salad he'd just made into the refrigerator to chill.

"Perfect timing," he murmured, then jogged to the front door, opened it and smiled. "Come on in."

"Sorry I can't stay," Trish said breezily as she shoved the thick Spirit file into his chest. He struggled to catch it.

"What's this?" Adam said, taken aback. "Why can't you stay?"

"I just remembered a previous engagement," she said through clenched teeth. "Oh, and by the way, Brenda said to say hi."

"What?" Adam shook his head. "Who's Brenda?"

"Oh, that's nice," she said tightly. "You date so many women, you can't even remember their names."

"No, I—"

"And she was so disappointed you weren't there. Here's her card. You be sure to call her for a good time. Oh, hey, maybe she'd like to come over for dinner."

"Trish, this is ridiculous. What's going on?"

"I've had my eyes opened." She seemed to deflate before his eyes. "Never mind. It's not your fault. It's mine. I never should've gotten involved. It was wrong. You're my boss."

"That doesn't matter," he insisted. "Please, Trish, don't—"

"Good night, Adam."

"Wait. Will I at least see you Monday?"

She sniffed. "I told you I wasn't going to leave you in the lurch. I don't go back on my word."

Adam couldn't be sure but he thought she looked close to tears. He grabbed her hand. "Trish, I don't know what happened but we can—"

"No. I'm sorry." She pulled her hand free and backed away from him. "I can't. I just can't do it."

"Move it a little more to the left, boys," Sally said, and Adam and Brandon groaned in unison. "I think it'll look beautiful centered on the window, don't you?"

"Yeah," Adam said, straining as he moved the heavy love seat one more inch. Then he dropped his end of the couch and swiped his damp forehead with the sleeve of his denim work shirt. "See, Mom? It's perfect. It's staying right here."

It was Saturday afternoon and his mother needed to rearrange her furniture. It did no good to ask why. Sally often got a wild hair up her butt to move stuff around for no rhyme or reason. But, hey, it meant free beer and pizza for lunch.

"Hey, Cam," Adam called, "bring me a beer, will you?"

From the kitchen, Cameron yelled back. "No problem."

Sally bent her head to the left, then the right, closing

first one eye, then the other, trying to make sure the love seat was exactly where she wanted it to be.

Ignoring her, Brandon plopped down on the couch and yelled, "Bring me a beer, too, will you?"

"Already on it," Cameron said, as he walked back into the den, holding three icy bottles. He handed one to each of his brothers, then took a long, satisfying swig from his own.

"I think it's perfect, right where it is," Sally said finally.

Adam chuckled. "Glad you think so, Mom, because it's not going anywhere else today."

"That stupid little thing weighs a ton," Brandon groused as he sat back and perched his bare feet on the ancient wide oak coffee table.

Sally sat down next to him and patted his biceps. "That's why I keep you around, sweetie. Now, take your feet off the table."

He did, but rolled his eyes. "Can you feel the love?" Brandon said, and his brothers laughed.

Cameron took a seat in one of the leather Buster chairs that faced the small couch. Glancing up at Adam, who slouched against the wall, he said, "Everything go smoothly with the Fantasy ADA survey?"

"Yeah," Adam said, taking a long sip of beer. "Trish had everything written up the next day and we sent the settlement letter off to the other side. Bob Paxton should have the renovations done within two weeks."

"That's fast."

"Yeah," Adam agreed. "He was motivated."

"By anger, I'll bet."

"Exactly." Adam grabbed a chair from the game table and sat. Just mentioning Trish's name made him worry and wonder for the hundredth time today, what in the world had happened to her last evening. She'd gone running off and before he could even think to go after her, she was gone. Now he would have to wait until Monday to find out how everything in his world had gone south between the time he called her at five o'clock and the time she showed up at his place less than an hour later. And who was Brenda?

He missed Trish, dammit. Not that it meant anything. It couldn't mean anything. He would never allow a woman to become so important that she had the power to disrupt his peace of mind. But Trish was his assistant. They worked well together. And yeah, okay, he wanted to be wrapped up in her naked, hot body more than he wanted to breathe again. But never mind all that. She was a valued employee. Of course he was worried about her. And that's the story he was sticking to.

"So, how is Trish?" Brandon asked casually. "How're things going?"

Adam flashed him a look of warning but said nothing.

Sally perked up. "Who's Trish?"

"She's my assistant, Mom," Adam said tightly. As if she didn't know.

"Oh, I've spoken to her on the phone. She sounds so sweet."

Cameron snorted as Adam slumped over in the chair, rolling his eyes.

"Who's Trish?" Brandon repeated with a chuckle. "That's real funny coming from you, Mom."

"It is?" Sally said. She glanced from one son to the other, then shook her head in confusion. "I guess I don't understand your male sense of humor."

"Brandon's humor is a world apart," Cameron said.

"True enough," she said. Again she stared at each

of the men, no doubt in search of the real story, then homed in on Brandon, clearly the weak link in this scenario. "So why don't you explain to me just how funny I am?"

Brandon exchanged glances with his brothers, then shrugged. "Guess it had to come out sometime."

"Ball's in your corner, dude," Cameron said, then stood. "I think this calls for more beers. Mom, you want something?"

"Chicken," Adam muttered under his breath.

"Got that right," Cameron said with a grin. "I can't watch."

"I'd better have a glass of white wine," Sally said, but didn't take her eyes off Brandon, who was starting to squirm.

"Coming right up," Cameron said, whistling as he left the room.

"Now, what in the world are you talking about?" Sally said. "What's going on?"

Brandon squeezed her hand patiently. "Mom, we know you arranged the whole thing."

"What whole thing?"

"With Trish." He shrugged again. "And Adam. We know Marjorie helped. We know the whole story."

She cocked her head and stared at him in complete befuddlement. Adam's stomach was beginning to sink. His mother wasn't that good an actress.

Cameron walked back in and handed her a glass of pale, straw-colored wine.

"Thanks, sweetie," she said, smiling up at him. "I think I'm going to need it."

"No problemo," he said, and quickly moved out of his mother's line of sight.

She took a sip of wine, placed the glass on the side

table, then cast a meaningful glance at Adam. "Can you explain what Brandon's talking about?"

Adam frowned as whispers of worry fluttered inside him and couldn't be stopped. Had he been wrong? Was his mother really not playing games? Impossible. He blew out a tired breath and said, "Trish is the woman Marjorie hired to be my assistant."

"What happened to Cheryl?"

Brandon chuckled. "Oh, you're good, Mom."

"Cheryl got pregnant and quit," Adam explained.

"Oh!" Sally said, clapping her hands. "Well, that's wonderful. I should send her a gift."

"Mom, focus," Brandon said, sitting forward. "We know you arranged for Trish to work for Adam."

She blinked. "I did what?"

"We know you're trying to set him up with women. You know, so he'll get married and have children and you'll have grandchildren and—" Brandon waved his arms around. "You know, blah, blah, blah."

"Ah." Sally's eyes narrowed. "Blah, blah, blah. Yes. Well, it's true I want grandchildren, but I'm not sure... well, tell me again how I arranged for—what was her name?"

"Trish," Brandon said. His patience was wearing thin.

"Right, Trish." Sally looked contemplative. "Tell me again how I arranged to get her into Adam's office."

Brandon cast an anxious glance at his brothers, not saying aloud what he was so obviously thinking. *Could their mother's memory be slipping?* Adam almost laughed out loud. He had no such doubts. Sally Duke was smart as a whip. She was pulling Brandon's chain. He shouldn't be enjoying the show, considering it was his ass on the line, but he just couldn't help himself.

"Remember, Mom?" Cameron spoke slowly. "Marjorie arranged it for you. She got Trish in there."

"Of course." Sally nodded. "Marjorie's a good friend."

"Exactly," Brandon said. "So you're not denying you set the whole thing up?"

"Why would I?" Sally asked. "It sounds like a very clever plan."

"We wouldn't expect anything less, Mom," Cameron said.

"Thank you, sweetie," Sally said, then glanced over at Adam with a sparkle in her eye. "All this talk of women and plans and setups reminds me, Adam. Have you gone out with Brenda yet?"

Alarmed now, Adam stood. "Who's Brenda?"

"Yeah, who's Brenda?" Brandon asked.

Sally sat back on the couch, seemingly enjoying herself. "Brenda is Geraldine Sharkey's doctor's daughter."

"Geraldine?" Cameron said, as he leaned against the back of the leather chair. "Your friend from the hospital guild?"

"Yes," she said, beaming at Cameron, pleased that he'd remembered. "We play canasta together now. She wanted to introduce Dr. Brisbane's daughter to some nice men, so I gave her Adam's office phone number."

"Oh, crap." Adam glowered. The mysterious Brenda. *She* was the one his mom had set him up with? But that would mean... "She didn't call. She just showed up."

"But, Mom," Brandon asked cautiously, "why would you send Brenda when you've already got Trish working for Adam?"

Sally started to answer him, then stopped. "What does Brenda have to do with Adam's assistant?"

"Very funny," Adam said, and started to pace the floor of the den. "Look, Trish is working for me and I'm happy with her. I don't want any more setups, so you can call off your dogs. Send Brenda somewhere else."

"Is she hot?" Brandon asked hopefully.

Cameron burst into laughter and Adam just shook his head.

Sally pushed herself off the couch and met Adam halfway across the room. She wound her arm through his and said softly, "Adam, you must know I had nothing to do with getting this woman a job in your office."

"I know that now, Mom," Adam said, leading her on a slow walk across the room.

He believed her. Which meant Trish was innocent. She hadn't been stalking him or playing him or lying to him. And Adam had treated her badly. Dammit, she'd been a virgin. He didn't like the guilt that had reared up inside him. He didn't like knowing he'd been wrong. And he didn't like admitting that he wanted Trish anyway. Wanted her now even more than he had before.

"It sounds as if you like her," Sally said cautiously.

"Don't get your hopes up," he warned.

She smiled up at him. "Honey, I always have my hopes up as far as you're concerned. And you've never let me down."

He let out a sigh. How could a man argue with the woman who'd given him everything? Even her meddling was a gift, he thought, because without Sally Duke in his life, he'd never have known what love was. "Thanks, Mom. You've never let me down, either."

"Oh, sweetie, you're going to make me cry." She wrapped her arms around him in a big hug and Adam felt like a complete ass. He wasn't about to tell her how badly he'd treated Trish. How he'd seduced a completely innocent woman. Innocent in every way.

Later, as he drove home from his mother's house on the cliff, he thought about how he'd sweet-talked Trish, flown her off to Fantasy Mountain and plied her with champagne. The following day, she'd given herself to him. In his office. On the couch. And various other places.

He should've been disgusted with himself, but the memory of taking her on his conference room table caused him to harden instantly and he wanted her all over again.

He had thought Trish was a gold digger, a willing accomplice in his mother's half-baked plan, anxious to get a piece of his hefty bank account. But she wasn't who he thought she was. She was the real deal. To complicate his predicament, he liked her. A lot.

"Dammit," he said, pounding his fist on the steering wheel. He would find a way to make it up to her. He would take her out, treat her like a princess. He would explain his mother's mistake in sending Brenda to the office. Then he would make love with Trish all night long. All week long. Hell, all month long.

He knew it wouldn't last between them. It couldn't. Adam didn't do forever. He would eventually let her go, but until that moment came, they could enjoy each other to the max.

Nine

Trish was losing ground.

It had been almost two weeks since that fateful evening when the elegant Brenda had shown up with her perfect hair and perfect shoes and ruined Trish's weekend.

But by Monday, Trish knew she had to thank the woman for opening her eyes to reality. She had no business dreaming of Adam Duke when he was the one responsible for all the unhappy turns her life had taken. From that day on, Trish had been on a campaign to find something, anything the least bit incriminating that she could use against Adam. So far there was nothing, but she'd vowed not to give up.

Meanwhile Adam had sworn that it was his mother who had tried to set him up with the voluptuous Brenda. And Trish believed him. Adam had explained that his mother wanted him and his brothers to settle down, so she had resorted to sending every woman she came across their way in hopes that one of them might lure the men into marriage. And that was never going to happen, Adam assured Trish.

Trish had laughed along with him when he described his mother's tenaciousness, and she accepted his apology, not that he needed to apologize. But since he was offering, she was willing to forgive him.

But she refused to forget.

Trish opened a file drawer and returned two folders to their rightful place, then pulled the file cart over to the next drawer. Adam was out of the office and Trish was all caught up with her work, so she was using this time to re-examine the client files in the hope that she'd missed something important the first time.

But her mind kept going back to Adam's apology about his mother's matchmaking efforts and his cold insistence that he would never marry. It's not as if Trish were looking for someone to tie the knot with, least of all Adam Duke, but it made her sad that he'd grown up to be so contemptuous of marriage.

And yet, despite his cynicism, he had been nothing but thoughtful and attentive to Trish in the two weeks since that fateful night. She'd tried but couldn't dismiss the memory of his arms wrapped around her. Every time she thought of his heated gaze, her insides twisted into curlicues.

For two weeks Adam had been relentless in his campaign to soften her up, weaken her resolve and change her mind. He'd been inventive and sexy and sweet, and Trish's resolve was slipping fast. He was fighting dirty, captivating her with his charm and consideration. Just when she thought she had a handle on her emotions and could withstand his latest salvo, he would slip through her defenses.

On Tuesday, he'd placed a single white rose on her desk and said it reminded him of her own unique style and beauty. Then he'd kissed her gently and she'd practically dissolved in his arms.

Trish buried her head in her hands. She had to be strong. She had to fight, not just for herself but for her grandmother and all the people who really mattered to her. And she *was* fighting, she thought, as she flipped open another client file and studied the lease agreement.

But every time Adam came near her, she was betrayed by her own body. Closing the client file, she sighed. Perhaps it was time to accept defeat. She just plain wanted him.

Oh, she knew it couldn't last. He was clearly not the type of man to settle down, get married and raise a family. Not with her, anyway. Not with the shopkeeper's granddaughter. Even with her MBA, she knew she wasn't the type of woman Adam Duke would ultimately marry—if he ever married at all. He would marry someone sophisticated and worldly, someone with whom he could travel the world. Trish's feet were firmly planted on solid ground. She wanted to live here forever. Sure, she'd love to travel someday, but it wasn't as important to her as home and family were.

And someday, she vowed, she would have a home and a family, but for now, none of that mattered.

For now, for today, Adam wanted *her*. And she wanted him. So for as long as it lasted, Trish would savor his desire to be with her. She wouldn't dwell on the future. She would live in the present, enjoy the moment and hope that her time with Adam Duke would provide enough lovely, exciting memories to keep her warm for a lifetime.

It had been one hellish day. Trish felt like a limp string of spaghetti, beaten and boiled and flung against the wall. She'd done nothing all day but put out fires and quell skirmishes that had been threatening to become full-scale wars. She'd definitely earned her paycheck and that was always a good feeling. It was just too bad she was way too tired to enjoy herself.

Once Adam had left the office for a dinner meeting with a visiting developer, Trish had dragged herself over to the file cabinets where she'd taken the time to go through a few more file drawers. Despite her overwhelming attraction to Adam, she was absolutely duty-bound to do something for Grandma Anna and her Village neighbors. So she continued her search for a scrap of something, anything she might be able to give to the local press, some story they could dig into in hopes of embarrassing Adam. It didn't have to bring down his entire company anymore. She just wanted to find something that would bring closure to the pain her family and friends had gone through. She owed it to them.

But tonight she simply didn't have the energy to scour the files. Her heart wasn't in it, even if her conscience nagged at her. She compromised between heart and conscience and worked diligently for almost an hour, going through and checking each file, before getting discouraged and calling it a day.

Knowing she had nothing at home in the way of dinner, Trish pulled into the local grocery store on her way home and parked. Before getting out of her car, she buttoned her coat because the nights were getting colder now. As she locked her car, she could see her breath in the air, and it reminded her of that cold night out on the balcony at Fantasy Mountain.

She shivered, remembering that it was out there on that balcony that Adam had first kissed her.

They would be going back to Fantasy Mountain in two weeks for the grand opening. Adam had promised that the two of them would go up two days early and take advantage of the spa and any activities they wanted to enjoy. There was only one activity she could think of, and that was making love for hours with Adam in that beautiful room with the luxurious, fantasy bed.

With that image in her head, she almost floated across the parking lot. As she reached the door, an older man bumped into her and she grabbed him before he could fall.

"I'm so sorry," she said. "Are you hurt?"

"Nah, I'm okay," the man said.

Trish did a double take. "Sam? Sam Sutter?"

"Trish?" Sam said, then laughed as she wrapped him in a bear hug. "Aren't you a sight for sore eyes."

"Oh, Sam, I've missed you so much."

His laugh turned to a cough that grew stronger and more deep-throated until he was doubled over.

"My goodness, Sam, are you all right?" Trish thumped his back, not sure what else to do. "Let's get inside."

Sam Sutter was an old friend of Grandma Anna's. He'd owned the bike shop in the Victorian Village, two doors down from Anna's Attic. His shop used to rent bikes and paddleboards and roller skates to the tourists who walked to the beach along Sea Cove Lane. Sam had given Trish her first bicycle and taught her how to ride it. Every bike she'd ever owned had come from Sam's shop.

Her old neighbor looked as though he'd aged ten years in the last few months since she'd seen him. She hoped it was just the cold that had him looking so worn down.

Sam stood up straight, the coughing jag over, but Trish could still hear him wheezing.

"Sam, you don't sound good at all," she said as she grabbed a cart and led him down the dairy aisle.

"No kidding," he said, blowing his nose with a linen handkerchief he'd pulled from his coat pocket. "I caught one of those winter colds and I think it's turning into bronchitis."

She placed a carton of milk in the cart, then threaded her arm through his as they walked down the next aisle. "You need to get to the doctor."

"I know, honey, but I just can't afford a doctor these days. I'll buy some cough syrup and aspirin. That'll have to do me for now."

"Did you get a flu shot this year?"

"Not yet, but I'll try to work it into my busy schedule." He grinned at her. "You're a sweetheart, Trish."

"Oh, Sam, I miss you," Trish said, and squeezed his arm.

"I miss you, too, honey," Sam said with a chuckle. "We had some good times back in the day. That reminds me, I ran into Bert Lindsay the other day."

Bert and his wife, Tommie had operated an upscale hair salon and beauty supply store in the Village.

"How are they doing?" she asked, as she maneuvered the cart around the corner and down the next aisle.

"Tommie's arthritis has been bugging her, but she's got a good attitude."

"I'll try to stop by and see them next week."

"You know they'd love to see you," he said.

"I would love that, too."

Sam waited while Trish picked out the best-looking zucchini she could find, then he said, "Bert tells me you're working for Duke."

Trish sucked in a breath, then exhaled carefully. "Yes, I am."

"I knew you'd find a way to get to him. You were always a smart girl." Then his eyes narrowed. "It's probably not very generous of me to say this, but I hope you come across something we can use to get his nose in a twist."

Guilt pooled inside her and sent hundreds of tiny ripples of shame out to every cell in her body. Here was one of her dearest friends, beaten down and destroyed by Adam Duke and all Trish could say was, "Oh, Sam, I'm not sure I can do that."

He touched her shoulder in understanding. "That's okay, honey. We all just appreciate that you'd care enough to try."

"I—I promise I'll do what I can."

They wandered over to the cold remedies aisle and Sam found aspirin and a box of extra-strength cough syrup. "Whatever you do, honey, I know it won't bring the Village back. But it would be nice if Adam Duke just had an inkling that what he did to us was wrong."

"That would be nice," Trish said halfheartedly, then wanted to crawl into a box. She could barely look Sam in the eye, knowing she'd betrayed them all by becoming romantically involved with Adam. What would they do if they knew the truth? They were all such sweet people, they'd probably forgive her. She just wasn't sure if she could forgive herself.

At the checkout stand, Sam began to pull cash and coins from the pockets of his old coat.

"Hey, I'm buying this," Trish said, pulling out her credit card.

"Don't be silly, honey."

"But it's the company card," she said lightly, hoping he'd believe her little white lie. "We'll let Duke pay for it."

Sam let out a rusty laugh. "In that case, okay."

As they walked out to the parking lot together, Trish asked, "Do you need anything, Sam? Can I help you in any way?"

"Ah, honey, I don't need a thing. It's just been great to see you."

"Are you limping?"

"It's nothing." He waved it off as he grumbled, "Doctor says I need a hip replacement. Can you imagine them cutting me open to stick a hunk of metal into my hip socket? That's not going to happen."

"Oh, Sam." She shook her head. "It might make a big difference and get rid of the pain."

"Maybe," he muttered, then he jabbed his finger in the air. "Let me tell you something: getting old ain't for sissies."

She chuckled. "That's what Grandma Anna always said."

"Yeah, I know." He laughed. "I miss your grandma a lot. She was a pip, that one."

"I miss her, too."

"Here's my truck." He gave her another big bear hug, then she helped him open the door. "You take care of yourself, honey, and don't let that Duke fellow get you down."

"I won't." She held his arm steady as he climbed into

the driver's seat. "You take care of yourself, too. Get rid of that cough."

"I promise." He grinned. "We're all so proud of you, Trish."

"Thanks, Sam."

She waited until he was tucked inside his truck and had started the engine. Then he waved. She smiled and waved back, watching until his truck disappeared out of the parking lot. As she walked to her car, she thought about Sam and how much she'd missed him. How much she'd missed her Village family. She was so glad she'd run into him. So why did it feel like her heart was breaking?

Adam shoved another thick lease document into his briefcase. "Are we all set with the orchestra? I know the union guy was giving you problems."

"It wasn't a real problem," she said, brushing off his concern. "The union rep just wanted to make sure we'd be giving the band two full breaks during the evening and I told him we would. So, no problem."

Trish had taken charge of hiring a big band orchestra for the gala. She'd never negotiated a deal like that before, never dealt with union issues or artistic temperaments. It had been exhilarating and scary and she'd pulled it off without a hitch.

Adam tapped his fingers on the edge of his case, thinking. "What do we do for music during the breaks?"

She smiled. "I've got a fantastic DJ to fill in. He'll also do some introductions and announcements. I've given him a script."

"You're amazing."

"I know." Her smile grew as he laughed. "I mean, thank you."

"You're welcome," he said, and glanced at his copy of her checklist. "So the music is set. And the hotel's taking care of the red carpet stuff. We've got limousines lined up to take guests from the airstrip to the hotel entrance. Photographers are set. Lighting is good. All the entertainment channels will be there."

"We've even got an actual red carpet."

"Oh, yeah. Can't forget that," he said, chuckling. "I think that's everything. Are you finished packing?"

"Almost." She thumbed through the pages of her list. "Oh, I've got the company jet flying your mother and her three friends to the resort the morning of the gala, then they'll be back to take your brothers and their dates up in the afternoon."

"Thanks for taking care of that." He pulled her into his arms and planted a kiss on her forehead. "I'm glad we're going up two days early."

"It'll take two days to get everything ready."

"We won't be working the whole time," Adam said. He'd already told her he wanted this time to be a mini-vacation just for the two of them. They could do whatever they wanted. If they were in the mood for some energetic physical activity, they could go cross-country skiing or ice-skating. Or they could just settle into the spa, get a couples massage, or while away the hours in the sauna or hot tub. He'd already scheduled a manicure and pedicure for her. He'd insisted that her every wish was his command, as long as she was pampered and fluffed and ready for him every night.

Trish doubted she would spend much time being pampered, but she couldn't help the tingles she felt when he described what he wanted to do to her.

She only had one more thing to do before they left the next day. She'd been putting it off forever, but the fact was, she needed a fabulous dress for the gala. Knowing there would be snow, she'd borrowed Deb's down coat and gloves again. But she still had to buy a dress. She planned to go shopping tonight after work, unless she could sneak off before that.

"That's it," Adam said as he closed his briefcase. "I'm off to meet with the SyCom people."

She handed him a thin folder. "Here are your notes for the meeting."

"What would I do without you?" he asked, then pulled her into his arms and kissed her. "Mmm, is it too late to cancel the SyCom meeting?"

Trish smiled. *If only.* "You'd better go."

"Yes, ma'am." He grinned and gave her a snappy salute, then grabbed his briefcase and strolled out the office door.

Trish sighed as she stared at the mess on Adam's desk. She would deal with all that later. Right now, she would take advantage of Adam's absence and go find a dress.

Two hours later, Trish returned to the office, ready to get back to work. She'd bought the most beautiful dress she'd ever seen. Why that made her feel guilty, she wasn't willing to say out loud, but at least she'd found it on sale.

After taking care of all the work on her desk, she headed into Adam's office. Files were piled everywhere on his desk, papers were askew. There was spilled coffee and a half-eaten cinnamon scone still sitting there. How could he possibly work in all that mess and jumble?

She began straightening things, starting with piling

the many files onto the file cart. She tried to match the loose papers with the files they went with. Pens and paper clips went back in the drawer, the scone was tossed out and dirty coffee mugs were hustled down the hall to the kitchen dishwasher.

After his desk was cleaned to her satisfaction, she pulled the file cart out to the cabinets by her desk and began returning them to the drawers. It took her nearly an hour, but she had almost reached the bottom of the pile. She picked up the next file wallet and checked the name. It was one she hadn't heard of. Vista del Lago. Curious, she thumbed through the thin folders and pulled out a piece of correspondence to see what it was all about.

She got through the first short paragraph before she had to fumble for her desk chair to slide down and sit. She examined the attached notice addressed to residents of Vista del Lago, informing the tenants that they had thirty days to vacate before the building was to be demolished.

The internal company letter to Adam was marked "Personal and Confidential" and listed the reasons why the building should be torn down. It was close to the beach, so the property was worth millions. It was an eyesore with paint peeling and wood trim crumbling, so it would take too much work to restore it. The tenants were mostly senior citizens on fixed incomes, so raising the rent had proved problematic. Better to just evict the tenants and level the building.

Trish's hands shook as she read the details of the coldly impersonal Notice to Vacate, which gave the elderly tenants thirty days to pack up all their worldly belongings and find somewhere else to live.

The letter reported that the Vista del Lago site would

be the ideal place to build luxury condominiums that would garner an excellent return on the company's investment.

She didn't know how long she sat there staring into space. She was struck dumb, frozen, unsure what to do next. This was it, the perfect sordid information she'd been seeking ever since she first came to work for Adam.

Her mind bounced back and forth between pretending she'd never seen the letter and shouting its discovery to the rooftops.

Part of her insisted that the letter was none of her business. She should just shove the file back into the drawer and forget she ever saw it.

But how could she do that?

It was documentation, clear and stunning evidence that Adam's company was about to tear down yet another building—this one filled with defenseless, low-income senior citizens—in order to build something more pleasing to the corporate eye, something like high-priced luxury condominiums with a view of the ocean. Much better than the ugly low-rent senior housing that was currently occupying the space.

Trish's stomach was doing backflips and not in a happy way. The letter and accompanying notice weren't exactly a smoking gun, but they were just the sort of dirt the local newspapers would devour like hungry hounds. It might not destroy Adam Duke, but if the press framed the story correctly, it would definitely be a blow to his company's reputation and Adam's personal pride would probably take a serious hit. If the news coverage was good enough and the public outrage strong enough, it might even prevent the project from going through.

It was the perfect weapon. Trish knew it. But how in

the world could she use it against Adam when she was in love with him?

"No." The word shuddered from deep in her throat as that realization sank in.

Trish rose from the chair and paced around her alcove. Feeling trapped, she went into Adam's office and walked to the window overlooking the coastline.

"Oh, no. Absolutely not." She whipped around, stumbling blindly back and forth across Adam's office. She didn't know where to go, what to do, where to hide from the stunning realization that she was in love with Adam Duke.

Barely able to take another step, she collapsed onto the couch.

How could she be in love with him?

She let out a moan, then bent over and buried her head in her hands. It couldn't be. Please, not Adam. Despite his good qualities, despite the fact that he was her lover, he was still the man responsible for forcing her small family and her beloved neighbors out of their homes. He was the man who'd destroyed the beautiful historic building where she and her grandmother had lived and worked their entire lives. He was the man who'd replaced that lovely, venerable Victorian building with an ugly, soulless concrete block-long parking structure.

He was the same man who would do it all over again to the residents of Vista del Lago, if Trish didn't stop him.

She sat up, glanced around. Maybe there was a reasonable explanation for his actions. Maybe he didn't know the whole story. But that was ridiculous. The evidence was sitting on his desk. He had to be familiar with the file.

It was staring her in the face. Adam Duke was about

to destroy the lives of yet another group of innocent people.

Sadness crept into Trish's heart as the inevitability of her situation settled over her. She had to do something. She had to take a stand.

No longer sure of her motives or her feelings, Trish scanned the Vista del Lago paperwork, transferred it onto a CD and slipped the disk into her purse.

Ten

They descended the jet stairway onto the tarmac and Adam inhaled the cold, pine-scented mountain air. He could finally relax and spend these next two days with Trish, uninterrupted by the work that had consumed them over the last few weeks. He planned to keep her busy in bed when he wasn't otherwise pampering her.

She'd been quieter than usual during the plane ride but Adam chalked that up to her usual anxiety over flying.

"I'm so glad to be back," she said softly, staring out at the mountains they had just flown over. Then she rubbed her arms. "Oh, but it's so cold."

"It's going to snow." He took hold of her hand and led her to the waiting limousine. "The driver will take us to the hotel, then come back for the bags."

He bundled her into the limo and held her close. As the driver sped toward the resort, he considered the woman sitting next to him. He was proud of the work she'd done and didn't mind admitting that she made him look good. She'd been thrown into the role of his personal assistant and she'd exceeded his wildest expectations. She was a hard worker and a good sport.

But more than that, she was sexy as hell and he couldn't get enough of her. He was amazed to realize that he hadn't grown tired of her, amazed that he still wanted her every day and night. He knew it couldn't last, knew that he would send her away eventually. He couldn't say when it would happen, but he knew it would. For now, though, he refused to question the fact that he wanted to be with her all the time.

He hoped that when the breakup finally happened, Trish would understand and not take it personally. He would be careful to make sure she knew that it wasn't her, it was him. Adam had vowed, long ago, never to become too involved with anyone. He didn't believe in forever, certainly didn't believe in love. He didn't trust it. After all, people might say they love you and promise to take care of you, but then they'd dump you off at a hospital entryway and never return. He ought to know. People lied.

After all the pain he'd seen growing up, first in the orphanage, then in all those miserable foster homes, he knew it was unavoidable that people grew to hate and hurt one another. He'd seen plenty of damage done and figured that for most relationships, it was just a matter of time.

Sally Duke had been different, he told himself. The exception to the rule.

But romantic love was doomed from the start. He wouldn't let that happen to him. And he wouldn't let it happen to Trish, either. He didn't want to hurt her so he was determined to avoid anything that remotely resembled a serious relationship.

And Trish had "serious relationship" written all over her.

But for now, for the next two days, he was looking forward to spending time with her and making love with her. And what better place to do that than Fantasy Mountain?

After the elevator delivered them to the top floor, he followed her into the presidential suite and watched with amusement as she twirled around, trying to take in everything. The room was spectacular, if he did say so himself. And needless to say, much bigger than the one Trish had slept in last time.

The walls were constructed of blond wood logs polished to a high sheen, except for one entire wall that was covered in river rock and formed a wide fireplace and hearth. A forest-green suede couch and charming bentwood chairs and tables made up a cozy conversation area. The wide, rounded balcony stretched the length of the suite with doors leading out from both the living room and the bedroom. In the bathroom, a soaking tub was planted in front of windows that looked out at the snow-capped peak of Fantasy Mountain.

Trish walked into the master bedroom and saw another small fireplace facing the king-size bed, framed in willow branches. She turned and faced him. "I didn't think it was possible but this room is even more fantastic than the one from before."

"That's because it's bigger," Adam said with a grin.

"It's definitely bigger," she said with a smile as she wandered back into the living room. "It's also different because we're seeing it in the daylight."

Adam followed her, content to watch her enjoying

herself. She peeked through the gauze curtains, then pulled the cord to open them, filling the room with more light. "Oh, the view from here is beautiful."

She turned to face him just as a shaft of sunlight bounced off her back, creating an aura of shimmering gold and bronze around her. It made him realize that she was the most stunning woman he'd ever seen.

"You're beautiful," Adam said, unable to keep the thought to himself.

She beamed at him. "So are you."

"First time anyone's ever said that to me." He approached her slowly. "I hope you didn't make any plans for the morning."

"Plans?"

"Yeah. Come here." He yanked her against him and kissed her in a soul-searing meeting of mouths and tangling of tongues. Then, in one swift move he lifted her into his arms and carried her into the bedroom, where he laid her down on the bed, then stood and began to unbutton his shirt.

Trish sat up to pull off her sweater, but Adam reached over to stop her. "I'll do that."

"Hurry," she said in a breathless whisper.

"Oh, yeah." Her mouth was already swollen and wet from his kiss and so damn tempting that he had to taste her again. He knelt on the bed and swept down to devour her, his tongue plunging in and around hers. He felt himself grow even more rigid and had to force himself to control the need that was consuming him.

He reached for her sweater and pulled it up and over her head. The slinky black bra was a surprise and he grinned as he used his finger to trace the shape of her breast, then dipped beneath the lace to play with her firm nipple.

"Adam, now," she demanded, then closed her eyes and raised her arms over her head. The movement caused her back to arch and her breasts to rise up. Adam swore under his breath and quickly unclipped her bra to reveal her soft, round breasts and tight nipples.

"Perfect," he said, and bent to take first one, then the other into his mouth.

He moved quickly to whisk off her pants, then left a trail of wet kisses along her belly. He gazed down at the strip of black lace she wore and swore again.

"You're so damn hot," he muttered. With one hand, he tugged at those skimpy lace panties and caused a tiny bit of friction against her soft folds. Hearing her whimper ignited his blood. He reached beneath the lace and touched her center, then dipped one finger into her. "So wet."

Tearing the lacy material away, he replaced it with his mouth, first kissing, then licking and finally feasting on her.

Her incoherent gasps fueled his own internal fire. He ran his hands up and down her strong, sexy legs, then grabbed her shapely ankles and hitched them over his shoulders. And continued his relentless onslaught of her hot, moist center.

The sensation of bringing her to a shattering peak was almost too much for him to take. Desire, painful and urgent, ripped through him as he crawled his way back up to look at her.

"You are the sexiest, most perfect creation," he said, unable to stop touching her.

"And you're wearing way too many clothes," she whispered, and grabbed his belt buckle.

He laughed, stood and stripped, pulling a condom out of his back pocket and donning it.

He had a moment to register her rich, brown hair tumbled around her delicate features, and her long, lush naked body stretched out on the luxurious bedspread, before kneeling back on the bed between her legs.

Holding her gaze, he positioned himself, then entered her slowly and had to grit his teeth to keep from exploding from her heated tightness.

It was all he could do to keep the rhythm slow, to feel each stroke move deep inside her, so deep that he began to lose himself in her, lose all sense of everything but her beautiful eyes and her lush heat. As his movements gathered speed, he felt a bone-deep need resound within himself, but refused to question it.

Her legs gripped him high on his waist, opening her up and allowing him to thrust even deeper. Her breath grew short, her breasts flushed dark rose and Adam knew she was ready to climax.

"Come for me, sweetheart," he said, his concentration focused, his thrusts slowing, teasing, until he withdrew almost completely. She opened her eyes in alarm just as he plunged back into her so deeply he thought he might lose himself in her. He rushed to kiss her, to swallow her screams, to savor her mouth as he thrust again, then withdrew. Then again, and again. Her eyes flashed hot and dark and he turned relentless, driving into her, plunging, stroking, their bodies damp with sweat and heat, his need savage and unremitting.

He saw her eyes cloud over seconds before she shattered gloriously. He crushed her lips again, tasted her passion, her pleasure, her sweetness, and lost control. His body tightened almost beyond endurance as he emptied himself into her.

Two days later, the night of the gala was picture-perfect in every way. It had snowed that afternoon, turning Fantasy Mountain into a glittering white winter wonderland.

Adam and Trish had reluctantly slipped back into work mode several hours earlier. Now Adam stood at the top of the wide main stairway leading into the hotel and greeted each guest personally. Wealthy investors and their families, old friends, a number of celebrities, even a few of his competitors, were all arriving to enjoy the opening weekend festivities. Adam's brothers and their top executives were already inside working the crowd.

The paparazzi swarmed outside, their flashbulbs and strobe lights turning the evening sky to daylight. Television interviewers were lined up along the red carpet that swept the entire length of the long carriage drive entrance. Heat lamps were posted at intervals to keep the arriving guests from feeling too much of the chilly night air.

From where he was standing, Adam could observe Trish with her walkie-talkie and her clipboard, co-ordinating limousine arrivals and valet service. She wore her jeans and boots and a down jacket as she worked the lines, running from one end to the other. She would stop to give an encouraging word to one of his staff, then laugh at a photographer's joke. She had a knack for making them all feel as though she were one of them while still giving orders and keeping everything on a tight schedule. She radiated confidence and warmth and it was obvious that everyone working the event had fallen in love with her.

Everyone.

Hell. Scowling, he ran a finger in between his collar and his neck. Why was it suddenly so damn hot?

Sally strolled up to him and put her arm around his

waist. "Darling, everything is simply fabulous. The hotel is magnificent."

"Thanks," he said, giving her shoulders a quick squeeze. "You look beautiful."

His mother wore a high-collared white satin tuxedo shirt with a black taffeta skirt and cummerbund—not that Adam would know taffeta if it walked up and bit him, but she'd described the dress in excruciating detail on the phone earlier in the week. Her hair was all scooped up in some kind of fancy French braided style, no doubt to show off her shiny, dangly earrings.

Sally beamed. "Thank you. Isn't it about time you got things started?"

"Twenty more minutes," Adam murmured, checking his wristwatch to be sure. He waved to catch the valet captain's eye, then tapped his watch and pointed to Trish. They'd worked out the signal ahead of time. Sure enough, within seconds, Trish came running.

"I'll make it on time," she said, bounding up the stairway and heading straight for the hotel door. On impulse, Adam stepped into her path and grabbed her in his arms. He swung her around, then kissed her and set her back down, breathless.

"You've got fifteen minutes to dress and get back down here," he said.

"You're not helping," she said, smacking his arm. Then her eyes widened. "Is this your mother?"

"Yes," he said, turning. "Mom, this is Trish."

"We've spoken on the phone," Sally said, shaking Trish's hand. "It's so nice to meet you in person."

"It's nice to meet you, too, Mrs. Duke."

"Oh, call me Sally, dear. Everybody does."

"Thank you," Trish said, smiling. "You look so beautiful."

"Oh, you're a sweet girl," Sally said, patting her hair.

"Yes, she is," Adam said. "Now get going." He kissed Trish again and she laughed as he patted her behind to push her along.

"So, that's Trish," his mother said a moment later.

"Yeah," he said, baffled and annoyed over the sudden and very public display of affection he'd just shown the world.

"She's absolutely perfect," she murmured.

His mother's tone had him eyeing her suspiciously. "What's that supposed to mean?"

She held up both hands innocently. "I'm just saying she's a perfectly lovely girl. And Marjorie tells me she's a hard worker."

His eyes narrowed. "What else does Marjorie tell you?"

"Oh, Adam," she said, with a soft chuckle. "If you only knew."

"Mother."

"Don't frown dear, you'll scare the guests."

He shook his head, then he held out his arm for her to hold. "How about if I escort you inside?"

"I'd be delighted."

With his mother by his side playing hostess, Adam worked the grand ballroom for the next twenty minutes. His guests raved about the rustically elegant resort and its beautifully designed ballroom and conference space. They gushed over the guest baskets placed in every room. Trish and the guest-services coordinator had selected the items to be included in the baskets and Adam had approved. Champagne, fresh fruit, cheeses and snacks, free spa treatments along with items from the hotel's exclusive line of hair and skin-care products, and a plush Fantasy Mountain bathrobe and towel.

Adam thought about his mother's earlier reaction to Trish. His suspicions were raised anew and he realized he would have to put an end to his affair with Trish as soon as he and Trish got back to town. The gala would be over and his life could get back to normal. He supposed he would miss her once in a while, especially around the office, but that's the way it had to be.

Having made his decision, he studiously ignored the tightening he felt in his chest.

As he greeted the mayor of a small town north of Dunsmuir Bay, he noticed the crowd begin to murmur.

"Oh," his mother whispered. "She's stunning."

He turned but couldn't say a word as he stared across the room. Trish wore a strapless black gown that molded to her breasts and fell in a graceful column to the floor, yet managed to show off every curve of her body. It was classic and elegant. And outrageously sexy. Her hair tumbled loosely around her shoulders and a thin row of diamonds draped her neck, bringing Adam's gaze right back to her stunning breasts. She looked like a goddess emerging from the sea.

She'd never looked more beautiful, if that was possible. It was Brandon who greeted her at the door, introducing himself to her and escorting her into the room. He snagged her a glass of champagne from a passing waiter and stayed by her side and talked.

Watching her sip champagne, Adam's insides tightened at the memory of their two days of pleasurable solitude ensconced in the hotel suite. They'd explored each other's bodies all day and throughout the night, finally falling into an exhausted sleep as dawn broke over the mountain.

Then waking up to start all over again.

The memory of her legs wrapped around him, her body arching into him, her sobs of need, caused a physical hunger in his gut and his jaw clenched as he forced himself to ignore it.

Adam checked his watch again. He had to determine exactly how long he'd have to stay at the party schmoozing with his guests before he could take Trish back to their suite. He could barely wait to strip that incredible dress off her.

"At the risk of repeating myself, she's very lovely," Sally said amiably, tucking her arm through his.

He looked at her squarely. "She's also a great assistant—smart, loyal, highly organized and very talented." And gorgeous in bed. Which is exactly where he wanted her. Now.

Sally touched his arm maternally. "I'm glad you have good people working for you, sweetie."

Adam exhaled slowly. "Me, too."

The orchestra began to play a big band favorite and Adam watched Brandon lead Trish out onto the dance floor.

"Crap," Adam said. Why was his brother holding her so close? He was going to cut off her breathing.

Sally chuckled. "Why don't you dance with me instead of standing here scowling? Your guests are going to think something's wrong with the plumbing."

"Good idea," he muttered, and led his mother onto the dance floor.

After a few minutes of gliding around, Sally smiled up at him. "You dance beautifully, Adam."

One of his eyebrows shot up. "I'd better. I risked my life to learn the damn fox trot."

Sally laughed. To this day, Adam couldn't believe she'd forced all three boys to attend cotillion when they were barely thirteen years old. Once word got out at school, the Duke brothers became targets and the fights began. The boys gave as good as they got, but often came home from school with black eyes and bloodied knuckles. Rather than cancel the dance lessons, Sally briskly enrolled them in marital arts and boxing classes, as well.

Chuckling, Adam recalled that she'd also forced them to learn how to cook and do their own laundry. She'd always said she was determined to raise well-rounded men who would make good husbands.

Adam was happy to be well-rounded, but that didn't mean he intended to be anyone's good husband.

"Every woman loves a man who can dance," Sally said suggestively, her eyes glittering with humor as she glanced across the ballroom.

Adam couldn't help but follow the direction of her gaze. His stomach tensed all over again as he spotted Trish, laughing and flirting and all wrapped up in the arms of his own brother.

The song ended. Trish and Brandon Duke applauded politely, then walked off the floor together.

"It was nice to meet you, Brandon," she said, and was surprised to realize she meant it. She'd been concerned when she found out that the outgoing man who'd met her at the door was Adam's brother. But as it turned out, he was a big friendly bear of a guy and a surprisingly good dancer. A former football player, he was several inches taller and a bit stockier than his brother. A very good-looking man, though not nearly as handsome as Adam.

"Great to meet you, too," Brandon said. "Especially after hearing so much about you."

"Really?" she said carefully. "Such as?"

"All good things," he assured her.

"Now I'm truly worried."

"Don't be," he said, laughing. "Listen, I'm going to try those Buffalo wings on the pier as soon as I can get there. Thanks for the recommendation."

"You're welcome," she said. "I've never been to Buffalo but I think they're pretty close to the real thing."

"That's what I've been looking for," he said. "Whenever my team played the Buffalo Bills, we'd always go to the Anchor Bar downtown to get our fix. I haven't been able to find the real thing since then."

"I hope you'll let me know what you think," she said.

As Brandon continued talking, Trish casually gazed around the crowded ballroom and ultimately homed in on Adam. A rush of warm longing rose from her toes all the way up to her ears as she realized he'd been watching her intently.

He stood with Sally, who stared up at Adam with a look of glowing pride and Trish couldn't blame her. Adam looked incredibly handsome in his custom-made tuxedo, and Trish shivered involuntarily as she remembered how the two of them had spent the early part of the day luxuriating in the soaking tub, washing each other's backs and making love. Then they'd dressed slowly. She helped him with his formal bowtie and cuff links. He zipped up her jeans, slowly, inch by inch, his fingers gliding along the zipper's path, touching her skin and sending ripples of heated desire throughout her body.

They almost didn't make it downstairs.

It was crazy. They'd spent the last forty-eight hours doing almost nothing but making love with each other. But now, gazing at him from across the ballroom floor, she realized she wanted him again. Would the wanting never cease?

It didn't matter. Once she returned home, she would turn the CD over to the local papers and quit her job at Duke Development. Grandma Anna would be avenged and Trish would move on with her life.

But for now she didn't want to think about that. For now, for this moment, there was only Adam.

She was about to make her excuses to Brandon and go to Adam, when a tall, dark and dangerously handsome man stepped in front of her.

"I'm Cameron Duke," he said in a deep, rich voice. "Obviously, my brother's too rude to introduce us."

"Not rude," Brandon insisted. "Just being considerate of Trish's tender feelings."

Trish grinned at Brandon, then shook Cameron's hand. "I'm Trish James, Adam's assistant."

"I know," he said, and his mouth twisted in a cynical grin. "I was wondering why we hadn't met you before, but now it's obvious."

"It is?"

"Yeah," he said. "You're beautiful."

Trish felt herself blush. The Duke brothers were formidable, to say the least, and each one was more good-looking than the next. The three of them must've fueled the dreams of every girl they went to high school with. Smiling up at Cameron, she said, "You're very kind."

"No, I'm not," he said bluntly.

"He's really not," Brandon said with an affable grin.

The band struck up the first notes of a sultry samba and Cameron held out his hand. "But I'm a good dancer. Shall we?"

"Oh." She cast a furtive glance across the room and saw Adam talking to someone else, so she smiled at Cameron and took his hand. "I'd love to."

"Mr. Duke. I must speak with you."

Adam turned, then had to look down at the short, thin man who'd addressed him. The middle-aged man wore a wrinkled black business suit with a worn purple tie and looked nervous and uncomfortable in the midst of all the festivities.

"Yes? What is it?"

"I'm Stan Strathbaum, former president of Strathbaum Construction, now a loyal employee of Duke Development."

"Yeah?" Was he supposed to know this guy? Adam couldn't say why, but he disliked him on sight.

"Yes." The man's lip curled up in a sneer as he pointed to the dance floor. "Mr. Duke, do you know that woman?"

Adam tried to follow the direction he was pointing and stared out at the dance floor.

"Which woman?" Adam said, his voice reflecting his annoyance.

"That one," Strathbaum said, his finger jabbing the air as he continued to point. "The one in the black dress."

What the hell? Was he pointing at Trish? Did

Strathbaum know how close he was to being tossed out on his ass?

"What about her?" Adam asked.

"I don't know her name, Mr. Duke, but I'll never forget her face. She stormed onto a Duke construction site several months ago and threatened me with bodily harm if I didn't halt the demolition of some old building near the pier."

"Couldn't have been Trish," Adam said confidently.

"Oh, it certainly was, sir," Strathbaum said, and pushed his glasses up his greasy nose. "It was her. She was hostile and unstable and promised to take down Duke Development if it was the last thing she ever did. At the time I thought I'd have to call security, but I managed to drag her out of my office myself."

He'd heard enough. How could this little creep stand here, insulting Trish? Who the hell did he think he was? "That's a ridiculous story."

"I'm warning you, sir, that woman is a security risk." He folded his arms firmly across his chest. "The entire resort and all the guests could be in serious danger."

"What are you talking about?" Adam said, a hint of danger in his low, deep voice. "I'd like you to leave before I call security to help you on your way."

The little guy swelled up like a self-important toad, but still managed to look wary. "Sir, you may not like what I say but I'm telling you the truth. I demand—I mean—"

But Adam had stopped listening. Instead, he stared at Trish, willing her gaze to meet his. He saw her eyes turn warm, then cloud up in confusion, then widen in horror as she seemed to recognize the obnoxious but apparently *truthful* man who'd just revealed her deepest, darkest secret to him.

* * *

From the dance floor, Trish noticed Adam talking to a slightly built man who looked alarmingly familiar. Her steps faltered.

"Is something wrong?" Cameron asked.

"I—I don't know." But suddenly she recalled where she'd last seen that man and his prune-faced sneer. It was at the construction site where she'd gone to beg someone—anyone—from Duke Development to put a stop to the imminent destruction of her home. At the site, she'd had the unfortunate luck to deal with Stan Strathbaum, the man who'd insulted her, threatened her and tossed her out of his office.

The same man who was talking to Adam. He was even sneering now as he pointed his accusing finger right at her.

Trish's blood turned to ice and her world flipped upside down.

Filled with dread, she pushed away from Cameron. "I have to go, I'm so sorry. Good night."

She quickly threaded her way off the packed dance floor and ran from the room.

By the time Adam made it up to the suite, she'd already called the concierge to arrange transportation back to Dunsmuir Bay. She'd packed away her beautiful dress and hurriedly changed into jeans, boots and a sweater.

He stormed into the bedroom. "Who are you?"

"You know who I am," she said wearily, tossing her underwear into her suitcase.

"No, I don't," he said. "Not anymore. Was that guy right? Did you threaten to destroy my company?"

"Don't be ridiculous."

"Trish, you went tearing off the dance floor the

minute you saw me talking to Strathbaum. What else am I supposed to think?"

"You're supposed to trust me," she said weakly, as she threw her toiletries into a small bag and stuffed them into her suitcase.

He grabbed her by the shoulders and forced her to stop. "Trish, answer me. Did you threaten to take down Duke Development? Not that you'd ever have a snowball's chance, but did you?"

She exhaled resignedly. "Yes, I suppose I did, but it's not what you think. I—"

"Not what I think?" he shouted. "Hell, you just admitted it to me. What else am I supposed to think? Somebody tells me you were threatening my company a few months ago, then lo and behold, you're on my payroll. What the hell? Were you honestly trying to destroy me?"

"No!" she cried, pulling away from him. "I just needed something to—"

"What did you need?" he demanded. "Money? Is that it? Are you actually the gold digger I thought you were all along?"

She stopped and stared at him. "You thought I was a gold digger?"

He shook his head. "That's not the point."

"You thought I was a gold digger?" Trish repeated more loudly, then came up close and jabbed him in the chest with her finger. "Let me tell you something, you arrogant jerk. I don't care anything about your money! Your company demolished my home. You destroyed my neighborhood, my grandmother's store, her livelihood and everything important in her life. You left us with nothing but rubble. My grandmother had a heart attack and died when you tore down the Victorian Village."

"Wait. Victorian Village?" he said, bemused. "I remember that place. It was like a landmark."

"Yeah," she said, squaring her shoulders. "It was. Until you showed up. I grew up in that landmark. That was my home. The home your company demolished eight months ago. And why did you do it? Because Duke Development needed a *parking lot*."

"What? That's not true."

"Oh, yes, it is," she said heatedly. "You bulldozed our beautiful homes and shops and replaced them all with an ugly block of concrete. You gave us thirty days' notice, then you evicted us. You threw my grandmother and all of our neighbors out into the street. They were good people, good friends I'd known my entire life. And for what? For a slab of concrete! My grandma died of a broken heart and I hated you for that."

"Wait a minute," he said.

"No." She gasped for air and realized that tears were streaming down her cheeks. She wiped them away angrily as she rounded the bed and pulled the rest of her clothes from the chest of drawers against the wall.

Adam followed her every step. "Wait a damn minute. I don't do business that way."

"Oh, really?" She looked up at him, saw confusion in his eyes and wished she could believe in it. Wished she could believe in him. But the facts were there. She'd *lived* the truth of how he did business. Maybe if she showed him that she had proof, he'd stop the ridiculous pretense of innocence.

She grabbed her purse, pulled out the Vista del Lago disk and thrust it at him. "You take a look at this, then talk to me again about how you do business."

"What is this?" he demanded, holding up the disk.

She stared at the disk. "It—it's something I was going to hand over to the newspapers."

"Then why are giving it to me?"

She laughed sadly and wiped away more tears. "Because even though you hurt me ten times over, it turns out I could never hurt you. I wanted to, Adam. I really did. But I just can't." She zipped her suitcase closed and stood it upright, pulled out the handle, threw her purse over her shoulder and started to leave the suite.

"You're not leaving," he said. "I want to talk about this."

"No more talk," she said, her world crumbling with each step she took. She stopped at the door and shook her head in misery. "You don't understand. I've betrayed my grandmother's memory by becoming involved with you. I've let down my friends and neighbors, the people you ruined." Her voice dropped another notch. "I can't believe I fell in love with a man who could do that to anyone."

His eyes were arctic blue as he stared at her in disbelief. "Do *what?*"

"That," she whispered, pointing to the disk, then she grabbed her suitcase and walked out.

Eleven

Adam had never considered himself a coward but he'd been avoiding doing something for more than a week and it was starting to eat him up inside.

He stared at the CD on his desk. The one Trish had given him. He'd put off viewing it for so long now, he was beginning to feel like a damn fool.

At first he hadn't wanted to look at it because he was just plain furious. At Trish, naturally. But also at himself for being sucked in by a woman who'd lied the entire time she'd been with him, then tried to blame him for her lies. He refused to accept that he'd been hurt by her betrayal. That was his mother's brilliant theory, once she realized Trish had left. Adam had less than politely cut her off, tersely explaining that no, he'd just been righteously pissed off.

The night Trish walked out on him, the night of the Fantasy Mountain gala opening, Adam had barely managed to return to the party where he maintained a semblance of civility—until he was ready to crack.

Once he was back home in Dunsmuir Bay, he'd buried himself in his office and worked day and night on other projects, other resorts, other deals. He had a business to run and didn't need some beautiful, treacherous woman running around distracting him. Even though every time he passed the desk where Trish usually sat, something inside him fisted in pain—that wasn't the point.

He knew his mother was concerned about him, but he couldn't deal with that right now. His brothers were another story. They'd made no bones about wanting to smack him out of this mood he was in, so they would occasionally show up at his house and drag him out for beers or otherwise try to cajole him into having some fun. One night, they showed up in his office with a twelve-pack and proceeded to berate him into easing up on the senior staff, some of whom had apparently been whining that Adam was taking out his problems on them.

Adam's solution had been succinct. They could suck it up. That's why they got paid the big bucks.

And besides, Adam wasn't the one with problems.

Meanwhile, Marjorie had quietly replaced Trish with Ella, a perfectly competent older woman who'd been with the company for ten years. She did her job, but didn't go out of her way to excel or make his life better. She didn't make him laugh. She never ordered him a healthy dinner on the nights he worked late.

"Like tonight," he grumbled, and reached for the phone to order a pizza. After three rings, he hung up the phone.

"Hell." Maybe he should order something more healthy from that upscale place Trish had found. He hadn't been sleeping well lately. Should he be eating more chicken? Or maybe a steak. He wasn't sure what he wanted, but it wasn't pizza.

The damnable woman had even managed to screw up his eating habits.

He shoved his chair back and stood by the window. Out on the bay, the full moon was reflected in the rippling water and the harbor lights twinkled in the distance. He swore under his breath.

It wasn't food that he wanted. It was her. He wanted Trish. Wanted her soft curves pressed up against him. Wanted her exquisite lips and tongue on his skin. And okay, he even wanted her clever mind solving his problems.

There, he'd admitted it. Satisfied? He slapped his hand against the wall of glass, then blew out a heavy breath. No, he wasn't satisfied.

Damn her for making him *want*.

He turned around and once again stared at the disk lying on the desk next to his laptop. He hadn't viewed it yet and he wasn't sure if he ever would. Why should he? She's the one who'd lied to him. So why should he believe anything he might see on that disk?

And speaking of lies, why should he believe she'd meant it when she told him she loved him?

Disgusted with his line of thought, Adam swept a piece of scrap paper off his desk and into the trash can. No, Trish didn't love him. No way. How could she love him and lie to him at the same time? Simple. She *didn't* love him, never had. Not that any of it mattered, he told himself. He didn't *do* love. Remember? Oh sure, he had cared for her. A lot. A small, pitiful part of him probably always would. But caring for someone wasn't the same as loving her.

And hell, it was a damn good thing he didn't love her because her betrayal would've hit him even harder than it already had. Not that he'd taken it that hard. It's just that, it could've been worse.

He eyed the disk again. Maybe he should throw the damn thing away. Or maybe he should return it to Trish. But he didn't know where she lived. Hell, he'd been sleeping with her and he didn't even have her address. He'd never picked her up for a date, never dropped her off, never kissed her good-night in front of her house. Didn't matter now.

He could probably get her address from Marjorie, although she'd been pretty annoyed with him lately. Still, he was the boss. He could get anything he wanted. Of course, even if he got Trish's address, it's not as if he'd go running after her.

"Oh, man," Adam muttered, spearing his fingers through his hair in exasperation. Knowing he wouldn't be getting any work done in his current state of aggravation, he shut down his laptop and left the office for the night.

That weekend, Sally Duke insisted that Adam come over for a special afternoon party she was throwing. He arrived an hour late to find the back patio deserted. When he walked into the kitchen, the only people he saw were his two brothers. Brandon stood at the stove, stirring and tasting Mom's homemade barbecue sauce.

Adam put the six-pack of beer and a bottle of white wine for his mother into the refrigerator. "Where's Mom?"

"She'll be out in a few," Cameron said.

Adam took a beer out and popped it open, then glanced around. "Anyone else show up yet?"

"Nope, this party's all about you, bro," Cameron said. Slouched against the kitchen counter, he took a pull of his longneck bottle of beer. "You've got Mom all freaked out. She can't stop worrying about you."

"Well, hell."

"Yeah. Which means we're going to have to kick your ass."

Adam rolled his eyes and drank his beer. "That's what this is all about?"

At the stove, Brandon shrugged. "Nothing personal you understand. It's our job."

"I do understand that," Adam said, picking up his car keys and slipping his sunglasses back on as he moved toward the kitchen door. "Enjoy the beer I brought. Say hi to Mom. I'll see you all around."

Brandon grinned. "And here I thought you'd be grateful for a chance to share your feelings."

"When pigs fly." Adam stepped outside and tried to close the door behind him, but Cameron caught it.

"You can run, but you can't hide," Cameron said calmly and stepped through the doorway.

"This should be fun," Brandon said, chuckling as he followed his brothers outside.

Adam stopped near the heated pool and turned to face his two closest friends in the world. "Guys, I love you, but if you come any closer, I'll have to kill you."

"Love you, too, bro," Cameron said, approaching him cautiously from the right. "But you're being an ass and we're tired of Mom bugging the hell out of us about it."

"See," Brandon said, taking a step toward him on the

left, "it's a matter of facing you down or dealing with Mom. You be the judge."

Adam had to admit they had a point. "Fine," he said, splaying his arms out. "Take your best shot. But I warn you, I'm taking you both down with me."

"As long as you go down first," Cameron said and rushed forward.

The explosion of water set off a mini-tsunami in the pool as all three brothers plunged into the deep end.

After some flailing and splashing and dunking of heads, Adam finally surfaced. He wiped his eyes of excess water and eventually focused on the pair of pink flip-flops standing at the edge of the pool. He looked up and saw his mother glaring down at him. She wore a goofy hat but her lips were set in a grim line and both hands were bunched up into fists perched on her pink shorts-clad hips.

"Hey, Mom, you're looking good," Adam said.

"Adam, I want to talk to you."

"Ouch," Brandon said. "She's mad."

"Yeah, that's going to leave a mark," Cameron agreed.

Adam sighed in resignation. He'd seen his mother's eyes before she walked away. She wasn't angry with him. She was worried. And that knowledge cut him in ways he couldn't begin to understand. He gripped the side of the pool and pushed himself up and out. Grabbing a towel, he followed him mother inside and found her in the kitchen, stirring the barbecue sauce on the stove.

"Everyone says you've turned into a bear at work," she said nonchalantly after a few moments.

"I've had a lot on my mind." He walked to the fridge and pulled out another beer, then sat down at the kitchen table, popped the top and took a long sip. "We're really swamped right now. Just opened Fantasy Mountain and now we've got Monarch Dunes opening in three months."

Sally sat down at the table next to him and Adam knew she was through beating around the bush. "Adam, what happened to Trish?"

He tried several ways of skirting the subject but eventually she wore him down, as she always did.

When he was finished telling his side of the story, she sighed. "Sweetie, even as a child, you didn't want to trust in love. But you're not a child any longer. Are you going to let Trish walk away, knowing you'll never be whole without her? Or will you find a way to convince her that you truly are the good man she once thought you were?"

"Let's get it straight, we're not talking about love." He realized his knuckles were turning white and loosened his grip on the beer bottle. "Besides, she lied."

"Maybe she had a good reason to lie. Did you ever ask?"

His jaw worked as he stared out at the wide expanse of grassy lawn that stretched all the way to the cliff. "No, I never asked. How could I trust her to tell me the truth?"

"Oh, Adam," Sally said. "Of the three of you, you were always the one who had the hardest time giving your trust."

"I trust you, Mom."

She sniffed a little and her eyes glistened. "Thank you, darling. I hope you always will. But more than anything else, I want you to trust yourself."

"I trust myself," he muttered. "It's the rest of humanity I have a problem with."

She laughed. "You're going to have to let that go." Sitting forward, she grabbed his hand. "Honey, if you want Trish, you have to dig deep, find out what happened there. Maybe it won't bring the two of you back together, but at least you'll be able to go on, having found out the whole truth. Until you do, I don't know if you can ever be happy. And if there's one thing I want in this world, it's for you to be happy. And you know I always get what I want."

Adam chuckled as he squeezed her hand with both of his. "You scare me to death, Mom."

"Oh, honey." She jumped out of her chair and gave him a tight hug. "That's the sweetest thing you've ever said to me."

He didn't go straight home but stopped at the office instead. It was a quiet Sunday so he knew he wouldn't be disturbed. Sitting down at his desk, he picked up Trish's disk and stared at it. "Vista del Lago" was written on it, probably by Trish, and he absently rubbed his finger over the script.

Swearing under his breath, he shoved the disk into his laptop and viewed the two pages of scanned documents.

When he was finished, Adam swiped his hand across his face. What the hell?

The letterhead was Duke Development's but he didn't recognize the name of the letter writer, Peter Abernathy. He logged in and used his special admin password to look up Abernathy's employment background and his record with DDI. The man had been president of Abernathy Construction up until a few months ago when Duke bought him out.

While Adam was logged on, he decided to look up

the same information on Stan Strathbaum. Turned out, Strathbaum had a background similar to Abernathy's. He'd been head of his own small company, Strathbaum Ltd., until Duke bought him out eight months ago.

After reading both men's employment histories, along with the DDI due diligence reports, Adam spent some quality Google time in order to get more information on both men and their business practices, as well as some details regarding certain historical landmarks in Dunsmuir Bay.

Finally, he sat back in his chair and thought about what he'd learned. For a long time, he stared out at the horizon where the pale blue sky met the cobalt blue of the ocean. He could now understand why Trish had been so upset by the thought that Adam would approve the plan to tear down Vista del Lago. She must've experienced a painful sense of déjà vu when she'd read that letter and notice, thinking Adam was out to destroy another small community of friends and neighbors, just like hers, all over again.

But what she didn't know was that Adam had never approved the Vista del Lago teardown. He never would. He didn't operate that way—not that she would ever believe him. And furthermore, he never would've approved the destruction of the Victorian Village if he'd known about it. That one had slipped through the cracks. Or rather, Strathbaum had shoved it through the cracks. The slimy little creep had rushed the demolition through before anyone at Duke could make a decision on the property one way or the other. And as furious as he was at the little toad, Adam had to admit that he was culpable, too. His company, his mistake. The mistake being that he hadn't been paying close enough attention. He'd taken his eye off the ball and people had been hurt.

With ruthless calm, he made a note to fire Strathbaum on Monday. Adam and his brothers didn't need someone like that working for Duke Development. But as satisfying as firing the man would be, it wouldn't bring back Trish's home or her grandmother. There was nothing he could do about the past. But there was plenty he could do about the future.

Trish drove to the hospital and handed the vase filled with two dozen perfect red roses to the clerk at the front desk. "Please give them to someone who needs them."

"They're so beautiful," the admissions clerk exclaimed. "But that's the third bouquet this week. Is it your birthday?"

"Not exactly," she hedged, then smiled. "Enjoy."

Actually, the bouquet of red roses was the fifth arrangement she'd received this week. Day one was daisies. They were so cheerful, she hadn't had the heart to give them away. Day two, pink roses. Day three, a beautiful spring bouquet. Trish had spent half the day mooning over that one before deciding it would be perfect for cheering up a sick hospital patient. Day four, shiny balloons and homemade chocolate-chip cookies. One balloon said, "I Miss You." She couldn't bear to give that one to the hospital so it was still bobbing around her tiny living room. How many more gifts and flowers would Adam send before he gave up and left her alone?

He'd called, too. Two, three times a day. She'd refused to answer or call him back. It was torturous enough just hearing his voice on her answering machine. If she actually spoke with him, how would she ever be able to block him from her mind and heart?

She should've been happy she'd proved him to be the bad guy she always knew he was. But she wasn't happy. She was miserable.

She pulled the car over and parked across the street from the pier. There weren't many tourists because it was winter, but the sun was still warm enough that she pulled a hat over her hair before walking across to the pier.

After buying a small box of caramel corn, she took the old wooden stairs down to the beach. The waves were forceful and the air was crisp and cold. She could smell the salt, feel the slight spray on her skin. She tried to think of happier times. Before Adam. She couldn't think about him because it hurt too much to wonder what might have been.

Was she being maudlin by coming down here? It was so close, only a block away from where the Victorian Village had stood. Now there was an ugly gray parking structure standing in its place, but Trish refused to look at it.

As she skipped through the waves that washed onto the shore, she thought of Grandma Anna, the only family she'd ever had. She barely remembered her father—killed in Operation Desert Storm when she was a little girl. Her mother died when Trish was nine and she and Grandma Anna mourned the loss together and grew to depend on each other.

Her grandmother had been her closest friend, her advisor, her teacher, her parent. Now she had no one, and it hurt so deeply to know that she was alone in the world. No family, no loved ones. Well, there was one man she loved, still. Even though he'd hurt her badly. She'd thought there was no greater pain than when Grandma Anna died, but she was wrong.

Losing Adam hurt even more.

She wasn't sure why it hurt so much. He'd never really been hers, after all. And she'd known his true nature all along. So why did it hurt so much now that she was alone again?

It had been three weeks since that fateful night at the Fantasy Mountain gala when that hideous man had spoken to Adam. If only she'd been able to stop him. If only Adam hadn't believed him. If only. Trish was sick and tired of moaning and groaning about things she couldn't change, things that could never be.

Such as the fact that she'd actually told Adam that she loved him. And he'd returned the favor by staring daggers at her as she walked out the door.

Oh, it was too humiliating to think about.

"So don't think about it," she grumbled, kicking up sand. "Do something. You need a job. You need to get on with your life. You need to do something about Grandma Anna's things."

She'd wondered what Grandma Anna would say about Trish falling in love with Adam, and now some words came to her mind. "Don't be ashamed for loving well."

Tears prickled her eyes. No, she wouldn't be ashamed. But it was definitely time to stop wallowing. She'd given love her best shot and she'd grieved over it. Now it was time to pick herself up, dust herself off and all that other stuff. What she needed was closure.

"That's a one-of-a-kind item," Trish said, wrestling the small treasure back from the woman who'd picked it up and shaken it. "An eighteenth-century pillbox. French, hand-painted with real pearls lining the edges. The cameo is carved ivory, inlaid on amber."

"Does it come in red?" the woman asked.

Trish wanted to smack her but resisted, much to her credit, she thought. Honestly, she'd wanted to smack so many of the people she'd dealt with today.

She didn't know what was wrong with her. She wasn't usually so short-tempered. She could understand people wanting a bargain, but didn't anyone in the world want something of quality that would last a lifetime or even longer?

Maybe it had been a mistake renting a booth at the local antique swap mart, but she'd decided she needed to sell Grandma Anna's antiques and collectibles, which had been in storage for the past seven months. She'd thought for a while that she would open another antiques store. After all, the reason she'd gone for her MBA, with a concentration in retail management, in the first place was to bring the Victorian Village shops into the twenty-first century. She'd had so many great marketing ideas for the whole neighborhood group, starting with obtaining the historical landmark designation.

So much for that pipe dream. It was time to move on with her life, time to clear away the clutter, but it still broke her heart to think of her grandmother's beautiful treasures going to somebody who didn't know a pillbox from a pop tart. She began to straighten the items on the back shelf.

"How much for everything you've got?" a man asked.

Adam.

Trish didn't have to turn around to know it was him. Every part of her knew it was him, including her stomach, which was performing somersaults at the sound of his voice.

It was vain, but her first thought was that she really

wished she'd worn something prettier instead of the T-shirt and jeans she'd decided to wear today. It was dirty business, setting up the booth every day, although visitors didn't seem to care much what anybody wore in the vast tented hall of the old fairgrounds.

She turned and took a moment to drink him in. Oh, God, would she always want to swoon whenever she saw him? Today he looked incredibly handsome in his high-powered suit and tie, even better than he looked in the dreams that continued to haunt her every night. Her throat was suddenly so dry that she grabbed her water bottle and gulped down the liquid. It barely quenched her thirst and didn't do a thing to calm her stuttering heart.

She forced herself to take even steps until she stood in front of him, separated only by the table filled with Grandma Anna's vast collection of antique pillboxes. With her chin rigid, she looked him in the eye and said, "I'm afraid you can't afford it."

His eyes narrowed as he stared back at her for what felt like minutes. Then he began to grin, slowly, calculatedly. Damn that cockeyed grin of his! It never failed to send her nerve endings spinning out of control.

"Hello, Trish," he said, his voice still as deep and sexy as she remembered. "You look good."

Well, she knew that was a lie, but it was a kind one. "What are you doing here, Adam?"

"Looking for a treasure," he said, gazing straight into her eyes.

She swallowed. Could he hear her heart breaking? Had he come to destroy her once again? It wouldn't take much.

"Look, Trish. I understand that I hurt you. I know

you don't trust me as far as you can throw me, but we need to talk and I need to show you something."

She sucked in a breath. "Adam, there's nothing you can show me or tell me that would change anything."

"I know you think so, but I want you—no, I need you—to give me a chance to change your mind."

She sighed. "Adam."

"You said you loved me."

She swallowed. So he was going to play dirty. "Oh, you heard that, did you?"

"Yeah, I heard you say it, so you can't take it back." Not breaking eye contact, Adam shoved the tables of knickknacks and collectibles aside and stepped inside her booth. In her space. Breathing her air. "I know you, Trish. You never would've said you loved me if you didn't mean it. Did you mean it, Trish?"

She tossed her hair back. "You thought I was lying about everything else. Why not that, too?"

"Let's just agree that I was an idiot."

"Okay, I can agree on that," she said, biting back a smile.

"I want you back, Trish."

Almost as quickly as it came, her smile was replaced by a frown. "Adam, it would never work between us. We're too different. You're wealthy and powerful and I'm just…me."

He took a step closer and said quietly, "I was dumped outside a hospital when I was two years old."

She hadn't known that and instantly, her heart wept for that tiny abandoned boy. "Oh, Adam."

"Believe me, Trish," he said. "My brothers and I have built a business and I'm proud of what I've done with my life. But I'm not all that wealthy and powerful on the inside. I'm just me. And all of me wants all of you with every last fiber of my being."

Tears threatened to erupt and Trish had to take some deep breaths before she could speak. "Adam, I don't know if I—"

He held up his hand. "I told you there was something I wanted to show you. Can you leave right now and come with me? I promise it won't take long."

Without another thought, she called out to her old neighbor, Sam, who was helping his friend Howie repair bikes in Howie's booth across the aisle. "Sam, can you watch my booth for a little while?"

Sam looked up and winked at them. "Sure, honey. You go on. I'll take care of things for you."

Adam said, "Thanks, Sam." Then he swooped Trish up in his arms.

She let out a little shriek. "Is this really necessary?"

"I don't want you to get away."

As he carried her down the aisle toward the door, people called out encouragement and a few ladies applauded.

"See?" he said, grinning. "It's a good thing."

She shook her head. "You're impossible."

"I just know what I want."

The drive to the beach in his Ferrari only took a few minutes. Adam turned onto a side street and drove another block, then pulled to the curb in front of a row of six lovingly refurbished Craftsman-style bungalows. They had all been converted into small retail businesses.

Each house was painted a slightly different muted shade of sage green or terra-cotta. Flowers bloomed along the walkways and charming signs were planted in the well-kept front lawns. Each house had a porch where goods were displayed, and each had a private owners' dwelling attached to the back.

"Oh, aren't they beautiful?" Trish whispered as she got out of the car. "I didn't know these were here."

"I didn't, either, until I started looking," he said, wrapping his arm around her shoulder and pulling her close. "But they were exactly what I wanted."

She gazed up at him. "You own one of them?"

"I own all of them."

"You—"

"Or rather, Sam Sutter owns that one." He pointed to the house on the end. "See the sign?"

Trish stared, then read, "Sam's Beachside Bikes."

"Oh, my gosh," she whispered, her voice shaking. "He never said anything."

Adam smiled. "The old guy's got the kind of poker face that could make him rich in Vegas. Mrs. Collins owns that one. Check out those mannequins on the porch. By the way, she's quite the diva."

Just then, Mrs. Collins walked out onto the porch and waved a huge scarf in their direction. "Yooohoo, Trish! Isn't this marvelous?"

Trish choked out a laugh but said nothing.

Adam pointed to the last house down the row. "Tommie and Bert Lindsay have already started moving their beauty supply inventory into the place on the far end. And Claude and Madeleine Maubert want the one next door for their patisserie. I think a French bakery and restaurant like theirs will do really well in this area. This is a well-traveled area, close to the beach, with a lot of small, upscale businesses and pedestrian traffic. I ran some demographics for all your friends' shops and—"

She launched herself at him and he managed to catch her. "Thank you," she said, as tears streamed down her cheeks. "I don't know how or why you did it and you're probably insane for doing it, but I can't thank you enough for this."

He stroked her hair, kissed her forehead, then turned with her in his arms and pointed again. "Did you notice this place here in the middle?"

Adam had thought it was the prettiest house in the row, painted three different shades of muted green with beveled glass windows in front. The door was old oak with wrought-iron fixtures and the porch was wide enough for a table and chairs and lots of potted plants.

"It's beautiful," she murmured.

"Read the sign, sweetheart."

Trish turned her gaze toward the white sign that swung from a post in the middle of the lawn. She gasped. The sign read "Trish's Treasures."

She stared dumbly at Adam.

"It's not Anna's Attic, but it's all yours," he said. "If you want it."

"Oh, Adam."

"There's one more vacancy," he explained quickly, hoping if he just kept talking she would change her mind and take a chance with him. "That's in case one of your other friends from the old building wants to move their business here. I tried to track them down, but I haven't heard back. Anyway, whoever claims the last place, I'll sign over the deed to them."

"But...why?"

He pulled her back into his arms. "Isn't it obvious? Because I love you, Trish." His gaze roamed over her face as he took in every inch of her. "I want to make you happy, sweetheart. I swear, I never would've torn down your beautiful home. It's my fault that I didn't keep better track of what my company was doing, but that will never happen again. I hope one day you'll believe me."

"I do believe you." She sniffled as she tried to blink away her tears. "The more I got to know you, the more I doubted you had anything to do with it. But that man, Strathbaum…"

"I fired him."

She bit her lip for a moment, clearly conflicted, then said, "Well, I hate to wish pain on anyone else, but I'm glad he's gone."

He stared into her eyes, so green and misty. "I hate that my name caused you so much pain. I wish more than anything that I could bring back your grandmother, but I can't. I just hope you'll be able to forgive me someday."

She reached up and stroked his cheek. "I've already forgiven you."

"Tell me I have a chance. Tell me you still love me."

Her bright smile lit up his heart. "Of course I still love you. I never stopped loving you."

"Marry me, Trish. Put me out of my misery and say yes."

"I thought you'd never marry anyone, ever."

He grimaced. "Did I mention earlier that I was an idiot?"

She laughed as one last tear rolled down her cheek. "You did."

He rubbed away the tear with his thumb. "You changed me, Trish. I want to be with you forever. Say you'll marry me."

"Of course I'll marry you." She reached up and

wrapped her arms around his neck. "I love you, Adam. I love you so much."

"Thank God." He kissed her, then grabbed her in a fierce hug and felt the formerly empty spot in his heart overflow with love.

* * * * *

Don't miss the next romance by New York Times *bestselling author Kate Carlisle*
Featuring Cameron Duke
Coming November 9, 2010
from Silhouette Desire.

COMING NEXT MONTH

Available August 10, 2010

#2029 HONOR-BOUND GROOM
Yvonne Lindsay
Man of the Month

#2030 FALLING FOR HIS PROPER MISTRESS
Tessa Radley
Dynasties: The Jarrods

#2031 WINNING IT ALL
"Pregnant with the Playboy's Baby"—Catherine Mann
"His Accidental Fiancée"—Emily McKay
A Summer for Scandal

#2032 EXPECTANT PRINCESS, UNEXPECTED AFFAIR
Michelle Celmer
Royal Seductions

#2033 THE BILLIONAIRE'S BABY ARRANGEMENT
Charlene Sands
Napa Valley Vows

#2034 HIS BLACK SHEEP BRIDE
Anna DePalo

REQUEST YOUR FREE BOOKS!

2 FREE NOVELS
PLUS 2
FREE GIFTS!

Passionate, Powerful, Provocative!

YES! Please send me 2 FREE Silhouette Desire® novels and my 2 FREE gifts (gifts are worth about $10). After receiving them, if I don't wish to receive any more books, I can return the shipping statement marked "cancel." If I don't cancel, I will receive 6 brand-new novels every month and be billed just $4.05 per book in the U.S. or $4.74 per book in Canada. That's a saving of at least 15% off the cover price! It's quite a bargain! Shipping and handling is just 50¢ per book.* I understand that accepting the 2 free books and gifts places me under no obligation to buy anything. I can always return a shipment and cancel at any time. Even if I never buy another book, the two free books and gifts are mine to keep forever.

225/326 SDN E5QG

Name _____ (PLEASE PRINT) _____

Address _____ Apt. # _____

City _____ State/Prov. _____ Zip/Postal Code _____

Signature (if under 18, a parent or guardian must sign)

Mail to the **Silhouette Reader Service:**
IN U.S.A.: P.O. Box 1867, Buffalo, NY 14240-1867
IN CANADA: P.O. Box 609, Fort Erie, Ontario L2A 5X3

Not valid for current subscribers to Silhouette Desire books.

Want to try two free books from another line?
Call 1-800-873-8635 or visit www.morefreebooks.com.

* Terms and prices subject to change without notice. Prices do not include applicable taxes. N.Y. residents add applicable sales tax. Canadian residents will be charged applicable provincial taxes and GST. Offer not valid in Quebec. This offer is limited to one order per household. All orders subject to approval. Credit or debit balances in a customer's account(s) may be offset by any other outstanding balance owed by or to the customer. Please allow 4 to 6 weeks for delivery. Offer available while quantities last.

Your Privacy: Silhouette Books is committed to protecting your privacy. Our Privacy Policy is available online at www.eHarlequin.com or upon request from the Reader Service. From time to time we make our lists of customers available to reputable third parties who have a product or service of interest to you. ☐ If you would prefer we not share your name and address, please check here.

Help us get it right—We strive for accurate, respectful and relevant communications. To clarify or modify your communication preferences, visit us at www.ReaderService.com/consumerschoice.

SDES10R

HARLEQUIN®

A Romance

FOR EVERY MOOD™

Spotlight on

Heart & Home

Heartwarming romances
where love can happen
right when you least expect it.

See the next page to enjoy a sneak peek
from Harlequin® American Romance®,
a Heart and Home series.

Five hunky Texas single fathers—five stories from Cathy Gillen Thacker's LONE STAR DADS *miniseries. Here's an excerpt from the latest, THE MOMMY PROPOSAL from Harlequin American Romance.*

"I hear you work miracles," Nate Hutchinson drawled. Brooke Mitchell had just stepped into his lavishly appointed office in downtown Fort Worth, Texas.

"Sometimes, I do." Brooke smiled and took the sexy financier's hand in hers, shook it briefly.

"Good." Nate looked her straight in the eye. "Because I'm in need of a home makeover—fast. The son of an old friend is coming to live with me."

She was still tingling from the feel of his warm palm. "Temporarily or permanently?"

"If all goes according to plan, I'll adopt Landry by summer's end."

Brooke had heard the founder of Nate Hutchinson Financial Services was eligible, wealthy and generous to a fault. She hadn't known he was in the market for a family, but she supposed she shouldn't be surprised. But Brooke had figured a man as successful and handsome as Nate would want one the old-fashioned way. *Not that this was any of her business...*

"So what's the child like?" she asked crisply, trying not to think how the marine-blue of Nate's dress shirt deepened the hue of his eyes.

"I don't know." Nate took a seat behind his massive antique mahogany desk. He relaxed against the smooth leather of the chair. "I've never met him."

"Yet you've invited this kid to live with you permanently?"

"It's complicated. But I'm sure it's going to be fine."

Obviously Nate Hutchinson knew as little about teenage

boys as he did about decorating. But that wasn't her problem
Finding a way to do the assignment without getting the leas
bit emotionally involved was.

*Find out how a young boy brings Nate and Brooke
together in THE MOMMY PROPOSAL,
coming August 2010 from Harlequin American Romance.*

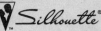

Brides

A powerful dynasty,
eight daughters in disgrace…

Absolute scandal has rocked the core of the infamous
Balfour family. The glittering, gorgeous daughters are in
disgrace…. Banished from the Balfour mansion, they're
sent to the boldest, most magnificent men
to be wedded, bedded…and tamed!

And so begins a scandalous saga of dazzling glamour
and passionate surrender.

Beginning August 2010

MIA AND THE POWERFUL GREEK—*Michelle Reid*
KAT AND THE DAREDEVIL SPANIARD—*Sharon Kendrick*
EMILY AND THE NOTORIOUS PRINCE—*India Grey*
SOPHIE AND THE SCORCHING SICILIAN—*Kim Lawrence*
ZOE AND THE TORMENTED TYCOON—*Kate Hewitt*
ANNIE AND THE RED-HOT ITALIAN—*Carol Mortimer*
BELLA AND THE MERCILESS SHEIKH—*Sarah Morgan*
OLIVIA AND THE BILLIONAIRE CATTLE KING—*Margaret Way*

8 volumes to collect and treasure!

HPI2934